PINSTRIPE
Parables

Discovery House PUBLISHERS

BOX 3566 • GRAND RAPIDS, MI 49501

*PUBLISHING BOOKS THAT FEED
THE SOUL WITH THE WORD OF GOD.*

PINSTRIPE
Parables

Searching Stories About Things
That Matter Most to a Man

David McCasland

Pinstripe Parables
Copyright © 1995 by David McCasland

Unless otherwise indicated, all Scripture quotations are from
THE HOLY BIBLE, NEW INTERNATIONAL VERSION
Copyright © 1973, 1978, 1984 International Bible Society.
Used by permission of Zondervan Bible Publishers.

Discovery House Publishers is affiliated with RBC Ministries,
Grand Rapids, Michigan 49512

Discovery House books are distributed to the trade by Thomas
Nelson Publishers, Nashville, Tennessee 37214

Library of Congress Cataloging-in-Publication Data

McCasland, Dave.
    Pinstripe parables : searching stories about things that matter most
to a man / David C. McCasland.
        p.   cm.
    ISBN 0-929239-91-1
    1. Men—Religious life—Fiction. 2. Christian fiction, American.
3. Parables. I. Title.
PS3563.C33743P56   1995
813'.54—dc20   94-44200
                                                CIP

Printed in the United States of America

95 96 97 98 99 / RRD / 10 9 8 7 6 5 4 3 2

• Contents •

• Introduction •

TWENTY YEARS AGO, a short fiction article profoundly influenced the way I read the Bible. "He Loved Me—He Loved Me Not" by Meg Woodson described the events of Genesis 1–5 through the eyes and emotions of Eve. The First Lady of Scripture spoke of her feelings in the Garden of Eden, her intimacy with her husband and God, and how her relationships were changed for all time by a single act.

That story sent me back to the biblical account with heightened interest. "Is that what really happened?" I asked myself. "I never thought of it that way before." It forced me out of the "beards and bathrobes" view of biblical people and events as being long ago, far away, and irrelevant to me. I studied Genesis with new eyes, trying to put myself in the story and find insight for the choices facing me.

In a sense, that story planted the seed for this book. *Pinstripe Parables* has a single purpose—to encourage you to read the Bible.

Most of these stories retell a familiar Bible event as if it were happening today. A few develop the theme of a biblical passage. None is intended to be an exact parallel of the Bible story or to "improve" on Scripture.

The human condition hasn't changed since the dawn of time. We still have wandering eyes, prodigal sons, and dreams of lives that count. We hunger for authenticity in ourselves and in others. The Bible confronts the timeless reality of our need with the eternal marvel of God's provision in Jesus Christ. That remains the greatest story ever told.

David McCasland

A MATTER OF ACCOUNTING

J. RICHARD SHELDON SAVORED the last bite of his veal cordon bleu as the flight attendant paused beside him.

"How about some more wine?" she asked pertly. The golden liquid cascaded into his glass as Richard loosened his tie and silently tried to guess the name of her perfume. "Passion?" "Poison?" "Obsession?" There were so many new ones these days.

She removed his plate and moved lithely through the forward cabin of the 747.

First Class on domestic flights was jammed with frequent flyers traveling on cheap tickets and free upgrades, but money still purchased a little elegance across the Atlantic.

They still put the pretty ones in International First Class, he said to himself. *I wonder what she does for fun? Wind-surfing, mountain-biking, roller-blading?* He imagined her moving swiftly and confidently along a beachfront sidewalk in California, vibrant with the exhilaration of living.

Beach volleyball, he decided. *That's all the rage these days. And, no doubt, she has a bronzed boyfriend with whom to play.*

His eyes lingered on the form moving within the cabin, dispensing tiny bottles of after-dinner liqueur. He had long since abandoned the fantasy of being slipped a phone number or hotel name during a flight, but he hadn't stopped looking.

Richard placed a laptop computer on the tray where his sumptuous meal had been and tapped in a few keystroke commands. A series of brightly hued spreadsheets winked across the screen displaying nothing but good news. He was used to that.

Dollar signs and digits had always yielded to his touch, even if women hadn't. While some people likened the ups and downs of the economy to the moods of a woman, Richard never accepted that comparison. The economy could be anticipated, manipulated, and even controlled. Female emotions? Well, they were, shall we say, less predictable. Less responsive.

He glanced outside at the full moon shining on a sea of clouds drifting below the plane. At 33,000 feet, the world was different from the snowy mess he had left in Chicago. Above the mess. That's where J. Richard Sheldon told himself he belonged. That's where he would manage to keep himself, come hell or high water.

The computer screen told him what he had suspected for some time. By razing his old warehouses and building a massive, state-of-the-art distribution center on the site, he could avoid taxes and create the potential for enough revenue to propel him so far into retirement he would never have to come out.

It had its risks, but what didn't? He had always lived on the edge—in life and in business—wagering what he had against what he could gain. It had cost him two marriages because neither of his chosen wives could understand why a man whom his peers praised as "a fantastic manager" could manage to think only about himself and his work.

Richard coped with the lingering pain by devaluing the quality of female companionship.

Even when I had women around me all the time it wasn't that great, he assured himself. *Besides, they didn't want* me, *just what they thought I had.*

At any rate, his future was all there on the screen in living color. Even the cyclical fluctuations of the economy couldn't touch it. It would take a global catastrophe to alter the future he had so carefully laid out for himself.

By this time next year he would be retired, yet making more money than ever before. He'd still be flying First Class, but to the sunny Caribbean, not drizzly London. And who knows, on that flight he might even find a tightly folded piece of paper with a telephone number being pressed into his palm as he left the plane in Barbados.

J. Richard Sheldon let the last of the wine slide smoothly down his throat and he basked in its quiet warmth. That would have to hold him until he reached his island in the sun. He laid the glass in the seat next to him, leaned back, and went to sleep.

Richard had checked, "Breakfast beverages only, just before landing," on his request card, so the plane was nearing Heathrow when the hostess gently touched his shoulder. She screamed as his head rolled to one side and fell limply onto his chest.

"Brain hemorrhage," the autopsy stated. "As he slept, sometime during the night."

Someone in the crowd said to him, "Teacher, tell my brother to divide the inheritance with me."

Jesus replied, "Man, who appointed me a judge or an arbiter between you?" Then he said to them, "Watch out! Be on your guard against all kinds of greed; a man's life does not consist in the abundance of his possessions."

And he told them this parable: "The ground of a certain rich man produced a good crop. He thought to himself, 'What shall I do? I have no place to store my crops.'

"Then he said, 'This is what I'll do. I will tear down my barns and build bigger ones, and there I will store all my grain and my goods. And I'll say to myself, "You have plenty of good things laid up for many years. Take life easy; eat, drink and be merry."'

"But God said to him, 'You fool! This very night your life will be demanded from you. Then who will get what you have prepared for yourself?'

"This is how it will be with anyone who stores up things for himself but is not rich toward God."

TROUBLE AT THE TRAINING TABLE

THE WORLD WATCHED Dan's country crumble one piece at a time. For agonizing months, television news brought the faces of grief and human despair into living rooms around the globe. The capital city, once host to artists, diplomats, and world-class athletes, now employed more gravediggers than university professors.

Powerful countries debated their role in the conflict and in the end did nothing to halt the ethnic slaughter. The United Nations proved to be a paper tiger. One by one, governments turned their faces from the horror just as people passing a terrible automobile accident are repulsed by the carnage. "Tragic," people muttered from Stockholm to Sydney, "but it's not our problem."

It *was* Dan's problem as he and the others bounced along a dusty road in the back of a battered military truck. Because of their families' wealth, they held out until the end, gambling their chance to escape against saving what they had. When the city fell to the rebel forces, they lost it all.

"Do they treat non-combatants differently?" someone in the truck wanted to know.

"Yeah. They give you a white blindfold instead of a black one at the firing squad."

No one laughed.

"What about the Geneva Convention?"

"We're a long way from Switzerland."

Dan's mind wandered away from the conversation.

Soldiers are taught what to do when they're captured in battle. But what about us? Civilian POWs in the hands of people who hate us. What are the possibilities? Jail? Torture? Re-education? Execution? Are we bound by a code of conduct? Ethics? Is it every man for himself? How am I supposed to know what to do?

Dan turned his face away from the others and tried to swallow the lump in his throat. It wouldn't go down. His entire future rumbled forward in a direction he could not have imagined a few years before. Rich kids weren't supposed to face this kind of tragedy, were they?

Dan glanced at his three closest friends before looking back toward the devastated city that represented everything he had known as home. Two streams of salt water traced arrow-straight lines down his face.

A few days later Dan sat at a long table with twenty other young men. Instead of the stench of a refugee camp, he and his friends smelled of soap and cologne. They wore clothes as nice as any they had owned before. The kindness of their captors caught them off guard. Instead of being thrown in a harsh prison, this felt like being admitted to a prestigious university on a full scholarship.

Their conversation stopped abruptly as the tall double doors swung open and an official-looking party of three advanced. A striking man with an accent addressed them:

"Gentlemen, please relax and be at ease. You have been selected for a special program of education and training. Each of you has been chosen because of your family background, physical appearance, strength, and mental capacity. You will undergo this training for a period of three years, and upon successful completion, you will enter the service of our government at a very respectable level. If you do not complete this training or refuse to cooperate, the alternatives for you in this country are decidedly less attractive. Enjoy your meal."

So that was the game, Dan thought to himself. Take the cream of the crop and put us to work for the victors. It reflected the reasoning of a mind steeped in the practice of absorbing conquered people into a new culture.

Of course. Don't put the strong and intelligent young men into difficult circumstances that would harden their resolve and incite rebellion. Bring us into the banquet hall and let us get used to living high at government expense. Place us under the tutelage of intelligent men who command our admiration and respect. Let us absorb your values and marry one of your beautiful women. In no time at all, we'll melt into your society like pats of butter on a hot pancake.

Waiters of diverse nationalities began filling the table with food. Filet mignon, fresh fruits, steaming vegetables, and freshly baked breads were set before them. Few of these young men had seen such a feast even in their own affluent homes. Wine with an announced vintage was poured for all. Its bouquet brought a heady sense of relief and hope to the young men who had expected harsh treatment and prison gruel.

Dan's eyes roamed the table and searched the faces of his three closest friends. He saw half-smiles and heard low talking as the food was passed quickly around, but no other eye met his. Were these the same guys he had grown up with?

They had adventured together since their first years of school, playing "Indiana Jones," hurtling over embankments on their dirt-bikes, and probing the limits of authority at home and school. Where was that spark of conviction and defiance now? Was everyone just going to accept this as fate's decree and embrace any belief as long as it produced affluence and ease?

Dan would have none of it. He filled his plate with vegetables and passed everything else down the table. He left his wine untouched and even had the audacity to ask one of the waiters for a glass of water instead.

Dan's choice of food and the set of his face did not escape the notice of the official who had addressed them before the meal. In less than an hour, Dan was summoned to the man's private office and told to close the door behind him.

"Look, son," the man said. "This is your life and mine that you're toying with. I was brought here many years ago as an outsider, just like you, but I learned to play the game. I worked hard to get where I am and I don't intend to let your narrow idealism ruin it for me."

"I'm not trying to make trouble for you," Dan said, "but certain things are important to me."

"Such as?" the man asked.

"Personal integrity and my faith in God."

"Religious fanatics don't last long around here," the official replied with a smirk. "My way is much more comfortable."

"I'll participate in your program on one condition," Dan said. "If you'll allow me to . . ."

"You don't make the rules here," the official bellowed, "you follow them!"

"Please, sir," Dan said quietly, "just hear me out."

It was the height of arrogance, in one sense, for a prisoner to make his demands known to his captors. But for some reason, Dan's words rang true, and the depth of emotion from which he spoke touched a nerve within the official. A faraway look came into the man's eyes as he listened, and he seemed to understand. Had he wanted to take the same risk years before?

Dan's one condition was the strangest training table request the official had ever heard. "Nothing but vegetables and water?" the official asked in disbelief. "Young man," he said, "I like you. You've got a good mind and a lot of potential. But on that diet you'll be emaciated and I'll be executed. Whether you know it or not, this is a serious business. If "the man" doesn't get what he wants, he comes after me. I have this terrible habit of breathing and I'd like to keep on. There's no way I can do what you're asking."

Still determined, Dan found a supervisor a few notches down the ladder and repeated his request. The man, apparently more adept at passing the buck, agreed to a limited trial period.

"Ten days," he said. "If no one notices, fine. If there's a problem, you're on your own."

The rest, as they say, is history.

DANIEL 1:1–20

In the third year of the reign of Jehoiakim king of Judah, Nebuchadnezzar king of Babylon came to Jerusalem and besieged it. And the Lord delivered Jehoiakim king of Judah into his hand, along with some of the articles from the temple of God. These he carried off to the temple of his god in Babylonia and put in the treasure house of his god.

Then the king ordered Ashpenaz, chief of his court officials, to bring in some of the Israelites from the royal family and the nobility—young men without any physical defect, handsome, showing aptitude for every kind of learning, well informed, quick to understand, and qualified to serve in the king's palace. He was to teach them the language and literature of the Babylonians. The king assigned them a daily amount of food and wine from the king's table. They were to be trained for three years, and after that they were to enter the king's service.

Among these were some from Judah: Daniel, Hananiah, Mishael and Azariah. The chief official gave them new names: to Daniel, the name Belteshazzar; to Hananiah, Shadrach; to Mishael, Meshach; and to Azariah, Abednego.

But Daniel resolved not to defile himself with the royal food and wine, and he asked the chief official for permission not to defile himself this way. Now God had caused the official to show favor and sympathy to Daniel, but the official told Daniel, "I am afraid of my lord the king, who has assigned your food and drink. Why should he see you looking worse than the other young men your age? The king would then have my head because of you."

Daniel then said to the guard whom the chief official had appointed over Daniel, Hananiah, Mishael and Azariah, "Please test your servants for ten days: Give us nothing but vegetables to eat and water to drink. Then compare our appearance with that of the young men who eat the royal food, and treat your servants in accordance with what you see." So he agreed to this and tested them for ten days.

At the end of the ten days they looked healthier and better nourished than any of the young men who ate the royal food. So the guard took away their choice food and the wine they were to drink and gave them vegetables instead.

To these four young men God gave knowledge and understanding of all kinds of literature and learning. And Daniel could understand visions and dreams of all kinds.

At the end of the time set by the king to bring them in, the chief official presented them to Nebuchadnezzar. The king talked with them, and he found none equal to Daniel, Hananiah, Mishael and Azariah; so they entered the king's service. In every matter of wisdom and understanding about which the king questioned them, he found them ten times better than all the magicians and enchanters in his whole kingdom.

WHEREVER YOU GO

"PLEASE STAND STILL, MELISSA. I can't pin this dress when you're moving around."

"Get rid of my little brother and I can," Melissa told her mother. The young woman gestured with her head toward a gangly boy in an oversize Harvard sweatshirt.

"The next rubber band you shoot at me is going around your neck, Freddy," the girl said.

"Muhlissa, puhleeze," the boy responded. "My name is Fred, if you don't mind."

"I do mind, and your name is Freddy. It's been Freddy ever since they brought you home from the hospital twelve years ago. Sad day that it was."

"At least I came from a hospital. They got you at the Humane Society."

"You little jerk—"

"For heaven's sake, would you two please stop it?" Marion Wilcox rose from her knees and tossed a package of straight

21

pins onto the dining room table. "Melissa, you are nineteen years old and this *is* your wedding dress. I realize that this is a stressful time for us all, but perhaps maturity could carry the day. During your last week at home, calling your brother Fred seems to be a small thing to ask."

"Ferd the Nerd, maybe," Melissa said, still trying for the last word.

"Do you need permission to get married?" the boy asked in a nasal whine.

"Not from you," Melissa snapped. "Look, *Fred,*" she snorted, "do you want to be in this wedding or not?"

"Of course I don't want to be in this wedding," the boy howled. "I don't even want to *go,* much less walk down the aisle dressed like a penguin and light candles with your future husband's tinsel-toothed sister."

"She's a sweet girl," Melissa said slowly, moving toward the boy.

"Of course, she probably won't even be here," Freddy continued. "She'll never make it through the airport metal detector with all those braces in her mouth."

"Fred, that's enough," Marion said. "Neutral corners. Time out."

The front door opened and a smiling David Wilcox walked unsuspectingly into the fray.

"Hey, it's the wedding party," he said with a broad smile.

"Hey," Fred said in a mocking sing-song. "It's the father of the bride. Dad, you look more like Steve Martin every day."

"I liked the 1950 version with Elizabeth Taylor and Spencer Tracy," his father replied.

"Dick Tracy's brother?" Fred muttered.

"Spencer Tracy. Won Academy Awards for *Captains Courageous* and *Boys Town.*

"I'll take movies for three hundred," Fred added with a yawn.

Melissa sighed. "Does he have to comment on everything?"

David Wilcox put an arm around his frustrated daughter. "When do I get to kiss the bride?"

Melissa turned her cheek away. "Right after you lock up the candle lighter," she said.

Freddy stood to his feet. "O.K. Truce. I apologize and promise not to harass you anymore before you ride off into the sunset with Prince Charming."

"If I could only believe you," his sister replied.

"Hey, trust me. This is the old reliable Freddy speaking."

David Wilcox extended a package toward Melissa. "Your things from the print shop, my dear."

Melissa eagerly opened the box. "Oh, these are beautiful," she said, extending copies of the wedding program to her parents. "They did such a nice job."

Marion Wilcox opened the folded parchment and read aloud: " 'Entreat me not to leave thee, or to return from following after thee.' It is beautiful. I wonder how many couples have used that?"

David Wilcox studied the page. "Thousands and thousands since Ruth first spoke them to her husband long ago," he said.

"Ruth didn't say them to her husband," Freddy chimed in.

"Of course she did," the father answered. "It's in the Bible."

"Bet you five bucks," Freddy said impishly.

23

"Make it ten," Mr. Wilcox countered.

"Twenty and you're on," said Freddy.

"Why must this child always insist that he is correct?" Melissa walked toward the stairs. "Are we through pinning this dress, Mother?"

"I guess so," Marion replied. "At least for now."

"I hate to take your money, son," Mr. Wilcox said.

"You'll hate losing your own a lot more," Freddy replied. He draped a leg over the couch as his father walked toward the bookcase.

"If Ruth didn't say those words," the father asked, "then who did?"

"Ruth said them," the boy answered, "but not at her wedding, and not to her husband. The Bible is quoted out of context a lot, you know."

"Fred, my boy," Mr. Wilcox said, "look for your wallet and get ready to pay off." He thumbed the pages of a large family Bible. "Joshua . . . Judges . . . Ruth . . . here it is."

"Start from the beginning," Freddy commanded.

"Ruth, chapter one," David Wilcox announced. He read nineteen verses then glanced sheepishly at his son.

Freddy grinned. "I'll take cash, traveler's checks, or a credit to my Visa account. And I'll take the Bible again for five hundred."

✳

Ruth 1:1–19

In the days when the judges ruled, there was a famine in
the land, and a man from Bethlehem in Judah, together with his
wife and two sons, went to live for a while in the country of
Moab. The man's name was Elimelech, his wife's name Naomi,
and the names of his two sons were Mahlon and Kilion. They
were Ephrathites from Bethlehem, Judah. And they went to Moab
and lived there.

Now Elimelech, Naomi's husband, died, and she was left
with her two sons. They married Moabite women, one named
Orpah and the other Ruth. After they had lived there about ten
years, both Mahlon and Kilion also died, and Naomi was left
without her two sons and her husband.

When she heard in Moab that the LORD had come to the
aid of his people by providing food for them, Naomi and her daughters-in-law prepared to return home from there. With her two
daughters-in-law she left the place where she had been living and set
out on the road that would take them back to the land of Judah.

Then Naomi said to her two daughters-in-law, "Go back,
each of you, to your mother's home. May the LORD show kindness to you, as you have shown to your dead and to me. May the
LORD grant that each of you will find rest in the home of another
husband."

Then she kissed them and they wept aloud and said to
her, "We will go back with you to your people."

But Naomi said, "Return home, my daughters. Why
would you come with me? Am I going to have any more sons,

who could become your husbands? Return home, my daughters; I am too old to have another husband. Even if I thought there was still hope for me — even if I had a husband tonight and then gave birth to sons—would you wait until they grew up? Would you remain unmarried for them? No, my daughters. It is more bitter for me than for you, because the LORD's hand has gone out against me!"

At this they wept again. Then Orpah kissed her mother-in-law good-by, but Ruth clung to her.

"Look," said Naomi, "your sister-in-law is going back to her people and her gods. Go back with her."

But Ruth replied, "Don't urge me to leave you or to turn back from you. Where you go I will go, and where you stay I will stay. Your people will be my people and your God my God. Where you die I will die, and there I will be buried. May the LORD deal with me, be it ever so severely, if anything but death separates you and me." When Naomi realized that Ruth was determined to go with her, she stopped urging her.

So the two women went on until they came to Bethlehem.

LET ME EXPLAIN

JUST LIKE THAT, one day she told me. "I'm pregnant, Joe. I know, I know, but . . . it . . . it's not your baby. Please, Joe. Just let me explain."

Explain? Hold my hand and spell out just how and why you've become pregnant by someone else? I don't think so.

Whatever it was I wanted from her at that point, it wasn't an explanation. An absurd line kept running through my mind like words from a B-grade movie script, "I guess this means our engagement is off."

What was I supposed to do? Give her a hug and say, "It's okay. We'll work things out"? Should I call the newspaper and ask them to reprint our engagement picture inside a circle with a slash through it?

I walked out the door as she begged me to stay, and I didn't even say good-bye. What happened next is still a blur. I recall walking away, slowly, with my head down. I saw no one and heard nothing. I must have walked for miles, trying to choke back an agony that came from somewhere so far down inside I'd never felt it before. Finally I started sobbing and didn't care who saw me.

Then I was running. How far would I have to go before my lungs and legs would hurt more than the pain inside? It must have been my fault. Why would she do something like this if I hadn't somehow made her do it? But what had I done?

It made no difference. I would punish myself for the wrong and take the blame instead of her. I couldn't undo the damage, but I could say it was all my fault. I kept running farther and farther from familiar surroundings with no thought of when I would turn back.

And then I was in a park, wandering from one bench to another, trying to find a place without people. Why did the lovers keep walking past me? What right did they have to embrace with their arms and their eyes in the presence of my pain?

Her betrayal refused to release its stranglehold on my mind. My fiancée. The girl I loved more than anyone in this world, carrying the child of another man. My feelings rampaged like a swollen stream—murky, churning, filled with debris. What kind of a world could create a hurt this monstrous? What kind of a God could allow it?

I picked up rocks and threw them as hard as I could into the dense growth along the nature trail. The slashing sound of stone tearing through leaves and twigs fueled my anger. More rocks, more harm, more hurt. And then I stopped.

Each stone traveled only a few feet into the foliage before dropping with a soft thump to the ground. Futile. Whatever I did was useless. I could expend all the energy and make all the noise I wanted, but it wouldn't change a thing.

My dilemma stood like the forest which had swallowed the stones of my rage. The trees seemed to stare back at me— fixed, unmoving, oppressive.

Explain? Right. Sure, go ahead. How could I even listen to someone who would do this to me? Why explain the obvious? What words could describe why I had been rejected and tossed on the scrap pile?

There was no explanation. No possibility outside what I felt.

Wasn't she the one I had risked to love because I knew she would never do this to me? We had promised to wait and had kept the fullness of our love from each other, for this?

Explain? I wish you could, Mary. I wish to God you could.

MATTHEW 1:18–25

This is how the birth of Jesus Christ came about: His mother Mary was pledged to be married to Joseph, but before they came together, she was found to be with child through the Holy Spirit. Because Joseph her husband was a righteous man and did not want to expose her to public disgrace, he had in mind to divorce her quietly.

But after he had considered this, an angel of the Lord appeared to him in a dream and said, "Joseph son of David, do not be afraid to take Mary home as your wife, because what is conceived in her is from the Holy Spirit. She will give birth to a son, and you are to give him the name Jesus, because he will save his people from their sins."

All this took place to fulfill what the Lord had said through the prophet: "The virgin will be with child and will give birth to a son, and they will call him Immanuel"—which means, "God with us."

When Joseph woke up, he did what the angel of the Lord had commanded him and took Mary home as his wife. But he had no union with her until she gave birth to a son. And he gave him the name Jesus.

THE WIMP vs. THE REST

IF HE DID IT, we knew it meant trouble for all the rest of us. But how to stop him was the puzzler. We couldn't just ignore him and we couldn't very well arrange his demise or even his disappearance. It was, as they say, a sticky wicket.

Pardon me. Of course you don't even know who he is. Or what we didn't want him to do. I'll try to bring you up to speed before we go on.

We called him The Wimp. You know the type. Physically he was ordinary enough, but he just wasn't one of the guys. He would never go along for a drink after work. Always had something else to do when a rowdy time was in order. On convention trips he stayed in his hotel room at night and read *Guideposts* magazine or watched Lawrence Welk reruns on PBS. You know the type.

From our perspective he was a climber; a guy who spent a little too much time with the boss to be normal. He never seemed to question things, never balked at the rules. He wouldn't think of complaining about working overtime or weekends.

He was just the kind of guy to ruin it for the rest of us. We were only trying our best to move things the way we thought they should go within the organization.

I suppose it was a basic difference in how we approached things. We wanted what was best for us. From our point of view, the company and its management existed for our benefit. The Wimp saw it the other way around. "The boss says this, the boss wants that, the boss knows best." Ad nauseam.

Anyway it was the most outlandish project we had ever heard of. A realist wouldn't touch it. Even the person who liked to do things that had never been done would have run from it. It wasn't the impossibility but the absurdity of the thing that turned us off.

It was like building a warehouse with nothing to store in it, or a bridge where no river existed. Picture a highway that went nowhere or a product that no one needed. The boss wanted it, and that was reason enough for The Wimp. It wasn't enough for us.

As long as we all stood together, the project was a "no-go." If the boss couldn't get anyone to do it, it wouldn't get done. If it didn't get done, then we would confirm who was really in control of things. If we could prevail on this project, we could do it with anything. Our heady sense of taking charge was exhilarating, challenging, and even a bit scary. But we were committed to hanging together on it. All except The Wimp.

At first we tried to ignore him, thinking his enthusiasm for the project would burn out. After several months it became apparent that he was coming from a position we didn't understand. Enthusiasm alone would have been consumed in no time.

But he was operating from conviction. And it seemed he had enough to keep the fire of determination burning for a long time.

We tried slightly veiled humor, barbed comments, and finally office ostracism, but nothing worked. He pressed on in spite of us.

We were carpooling home from work one day when Harold Green hit on the solution.

"Off-site," he said right out of the blue.

When no one responded, he said it again, louder.

"Off-site!"

"What are you talking about?" Curt Martin demanded.

"We move The Wimp off-site," Harold chortled. "Let him have his project, hire his staff, and do his thing away from the rest of us in the company. Out of sight, out of mind."

It was so simple it worked. We made repeated complaints about crowded conditions in the factory and then offered a proposal to utilize some vacant land owned by the company. The boss agreed to our suggestion and relocated The Wimp and his project to a site five miles from the main company operations. He was finally out of our hair.

For the first time in months, we began to go through entire days without mentioning The Wimp or thinking about what he was doing. We got back to living as we always had, doing business as usual, making money for the company. The Wimp and the boss had their little project together and that was fine with us. They could do whatever they wanted as long as they didn't try to get us involved. Talk about liberation.

One night, months later, on the way home from work, we stopped in for a drink at the Twin Rivers Tavern. The Wimp's name came up in conversation and we decided to divert our carpool past his project site just long enough to see if anything was still happening. It had been a long time since we'd even thought about him.

We drove to the top of a hill overlooking the place where The Wimp had been at work. I parked the car on the shoulder of the road, we all got out and peered into the valley below.

"Would you look at that!" Harold Green shouted over the rising wind.

"Unbelievable!" I yelled back.

We all pointed involuntarily toward what we could plainly see.

"Looks like he's got it finished," Curt Martin said, turning his collar up against the gale.

A raindrop splattered against my cheek and dozens of wind-driven droplets followed. I removed my glasses and the scene below me retreated into a nearsighted blur.

"Well, I'll be damned," I mumbled. "I *will* be damned."

GENESIS 6:9–7:12, 21–23

This is the account of Noah.

Noah was a righteous man, blameless among the people of his time, and he walked with God. Noah had three sons: Shem, Ham and Japheth.

Now the earth was corrupt in God's sight and was full of violence. God saw how corrupt the earth had become, for all the people on earth had corrupted their ways. So God said to Noah, "I am going to put an end to all people, for the earth is filled with violence because of them. I am surely going to destroy both them and the earth. So make yourself an ark of cypress wood; make rooms in it and coat it with pitch inside and out. This is how you are to build it: The ark is to be 450 feet long, 75 feet wide and 45 feet high. Make a roof for it and finish the ark to within 18 inches of the top. Put a door in the side of the ark and make lower, middle and upper decks. I am going to bring floodwaters on the earth to destroy all life under the heavens, every creature that has the breath of life in it. Everything on earth will perish. But I will establish my covenant with you, and you will enter the ark—you and your sons and your wife and your sons' wives with you. You are to bring into the ark two of all living creatures, male and female, to keep them alive with you. Two of every kind of bird, of every kind of animal and of every kind of creature that moves along the ground will come to you to be kept alive. You are to take every kind of food that is to be eaten and store it away as food for you and for them."

Noah did everything just as God commanded him.

The LORD then said to Noah, "Go into the ark, you and your whole family, because I have found you righteous in this generation. Take with you seven of every kind of clean animal, a male and its mate, and two of every kind of unclean animal, a male and its mate, and also seven of every kind of bird, male and female, to keep their various kinds alive throughout the earth. Seven days from now I will send rain on the earth for forty days and forty nights, and I will wipe from the face of the earth every living creature I have made."

And Noah did all that the LORD commanded him.

Noah was six hundred years old when the floodwaters came on the earth. And Noah and his sons and his wife and his sons' wives entered the ark to escape the waters of the flood. Pairs of clean and unclean animals, of birds and of all creatures that move along the ground, male and female, came to Noah and entered the ark, as God had commanded Noah. And after the seven days the floodwaters came on the earth.

In the six hundredth year of Noah's life, on the seventeenth day of the second month—on that day all the springs of the great deep burst forth, and the floodgates of the heavens were opened. And rain fell on the earth forty days and forty nights. . . .

Every living thing that moved on the earth perished—birds, livestock, wild animals, all the creatures that swarm over the earth, and all mankind. Everything on dry land that had the breath of life in its nostrils died. Every living thing on the face of the earth was wiped out; men and animals and the creatures that move along the ground and the birds of the air were wiped from the earth. Only Noah was left, and those with him in the ark.

HEBREWS 11:7

By faith Noah, when warned about things not yet seen, in holy fear built an ark to save his family. By his faith he condemned the world and became heir of the righteousness that comes by faith.

THE END OF THE ENDLESS HONEYMOON

T HEY WERE THE PERFECT COUPLE. If you'd seen them, you would have said so yourself. Body, mind, personality—they had it all. She looked like a movie star, a magazine model, and the most beautifully innocent girl back home all rolled into one. She was more than enough to send any man into yearnings of the highest magnitude. But deep in her heart, she knew she belonged only to one man.

He was no slouch himself. Intellectually he combined an insatiable desire to learn with a steel-trap memory that made him, not computer-like, but God-like in relationship to everything in his world. Besides that he was an artist, unusually creative and incurably romantic. Physically he had no peer.

You'd expect them to have the perfect marriage and they did. At least for a while.

For their honeymoon, a wealthy friend gave them unlimited use of a beautiful country home, completely furnished with everything they could possibly want. "Stay as long as you like," he told them. "I may pop in from time to time to say hello, but basically, it's yours." Along with the rent-free mansion came a check for $500,000.

Their spacious country estate was completely secure and totally private. Within it they were free to go anywhere and do anything they wanted. They could sing in the shower, turn the CD player up to "9," sunbathe, sit by the pool, or spend a day in complete silence and never worry about being interrupted.

Far from a static, boring existence, it held the opportunity to learn, experiment, work, create, and be fulfilled in ways the couple had never imagined. It was the only place where a man and woman could work or play and hardly notice a difference between the two.

However, there was one restriction. In the wine cellar an oak cabinet with opaque glass doors stood locked while hundreds of bottles lay on open wooden racks. During their early days of exploring the house together, they had discovered the cabinet with its half-dozen wine bottles inside.

"Remember what he said about keeping some of his personal things in locked cases?" she asked her husband.

"Sure," the man answered. "He said, 'You don't need any of those things.' Not you *won't* need, but you *don't* need. That's a funny twist. Like we might hurt ourselves."

"Well, it's not like he left us poverty stricken or anything like that," she concluded, running her hand over the top of the cabinet. "If we decide to have a glass of wine with dinner some night, there are certainly enough other choices available."

Late one afternoon, a man in overalls carrying a crescent wrench sauntered unannounced into the back yard.

"You startled me," the young bride said, glancing up from a paperback book.

"Sorry," the man replied. "I'm the handyman. Just here to check the lawn sprinkler system. Everything working okay?"

"We haven't noticed anything wrong," she said, carefully eyeing the stranger. "Comes on automatically every morning."

"Super," said the man. "Quite a place, huh? Your husband around?"

"He's on the patio, grilling some halibut for dinner."

"Yeah, thought I smelled something good. You'll enjoy a nice Chablis with that. There's an outstanding vintage in the oak cabinet in the wine cellar."

"How did you know about that?" she asked.

"That's where the timer boxes and the valves for the sprinkler system are," he said. "In the cellar."

"That's nice," she replied, rising from her chaise lounge. "But the cabinet is locked."

"Really?" the man said. "Well, that figures. That's where he keeps the good stuff."

With a glance at his watch, he began walking away. "Call me if you have any sprinkler problems. And enjoy your dinner."

She walked slowly around to the patio, gave her husband a kiss and asked, "How long till we eat?"

"Ten minutes, max."

"Let's have some wine tonight," she said, taking his hand. "You help me choose . . . from the mysterious cabinet."

Like two curious children, they probed the lock gently with the blade from his small pocket knife. Nothing. He inserted a screwdriver between the doors.

41

"If we can pry these open a little," he said, "at least we can see what's inside. Just a little more . . . "

Her face was turned to the side when the glass doors shattered, littering the floor with jagged shards.

"Honey, are you okay?" His voice trembled.

"I'm fine," she said, shaking tiny slivers from her hair. "What a mess. Well, now we can make our selection. I think the Chablis would be nice."

The wine was excellent, but somehow not what they expected. After dinner they tried to talk but the conversation stayed in the doldrums of facts, hungering for a fresh wind of feeling.

"I've been thinking about spending a few days at the coast," he said.

"Finished reading my book today," she replied. "Not bad."

"I haven't seen a good movie in a long time."

Finally he rose from the table. "Don't worry about the cabinet. I'll clean up the glass tomorrow, get the doors fixed, and everything will be as good as new. And one bottle isn't going to make any difference in that stash down there."

"There's probably a phone number somewhere for the handyman," she said absently. "He may know what to do."

They moved to the sofa but instead of snuggling close to him the way she always had, she found herself sitting at the far end, staring into the darkness beyond the picture window.

"Hey, it's no big deal," he tried to reassure her. "Don't worry about it. We can fix it. No one will ever know."

Genesis 2:8–9,15–3:9

The LORD God had planted a garden in the east, in Eden; and there he put the man he had formed. And the LORD God made all kinds of trees grow out of the ground—trees that were pleasing to the eye and good for food. In the middle of the garden were the tree of life and the tree of the knowledge of good and evil. . . .

The LORD God took the man and put him in the Garden of Eden to work it and take care of it. And the LORD God commanded the man, "You are free to eat from any tree in the garden; but you must not eat from the tree of the knowledge of good and evil, for when you eat of it you will surely die."

The LORD God said, "It is not good for the man to be alone. I will make a helper suitable for him."

Now the Lord God had formed out of the ground all the beasts of the field and all the birds of the air. He brought them to the man to see what he would name them; and whatever the man called each living creature, that was its name. So the man gave names to all the livestock, the birds of the air and all the beasts of the field.

But for Adam no suitable helper was found. So the LORD God caused the man to fall into a deep sleep; and while he was sleeping, he took one of the man's ribs and closed up the place with flesh. Then the LORD God made a woman from the rib he had taken out of the man, and he brought her to the man.

The man said,
"This is now bone of my bones
and flesh of my flesh;

43

she shall be called 'woman,'
for she was taken out of man."
For this reason a man will leave his father and mother and be
united to his wife, and they will become one flesh.

The man and his wife were both naked, and they felt no
shame.

Now the serpent was more crafty than any of the wild
animals the LORD God had made. He said to the woman, "Did
God really say, 'You must not eat from any tree in the garden'?"

The woman said to the serpent, "We may eat fruit from
the trees in the garden, but God did say, 'You must not eat fruit
from the tree that is in the middle of the garden, and you must
not touch it, or you will die.'"

"You will not surely die," the serpent said to the woman.
"For God knows that when you eat of it your eyes will be opened,
and you will be like God, knowing good and evil."

When the woman saw that the fruit of the tree was good
for food and pleasing to the eye, and also desirable for gaining
wisdom, she took some and ate it. She also gave some to her husband, who was with her, and he ate it. Then the eyes of both of
them were opened, and they realized they were naked; so they
sewed fig leaves together and made coverings for themselves.

Then the man and his wife heard the sound of the LORD
God as he was walking in the garden in the cool of the day, and
they hid from the LORD God among the trees of the garden. But
the LORD God called to the man, "Where are you?"

THE AD MAN'S NIGHTMARE

CONFERENCE ROOM, Wesson & Smith Advertising, Saturday, 7:00 A.M.

Before the meeting began I glanced down at a sheet of our company's letterhead stationery. The average man would have put his own name first in the company title, but my boss, Marc Smith, was nowhere near average. "Smith & Wesson Advertising?" he once replied to someone who asked. "The smoking gun of Madison Avenue? Have storyboard, will travel? I don't think so."

Besides, "Wesson" was Marc's father-in-law whose only involvement was a $5,000 loan made a decade before to help Marc rent an office and buy an old desktop computer. Mark repaid the loan in two months and the rest is advertising history. Wesson & Smith systematically lured major accounts from huge agencies who had owned them for years. The CEO of a big-three automaker shifted his corporate account to the agency and told his former ad agency, "When I compare your creativity to Marc Smith, it's like a dripping faucet next to Niagara." Marc cared nothing about his name on the top of the stationery. His concern was for the bottom line.

At Wesson & Smith, we all worked five days a week from 10:00 A.M. to 6:00 P.M. The routine never varied. Marc said, "We will get it done during regular hours, or we won't do it. I intend to have a life now, not when I retire." There were no all-nighters, no weekends, no deadlines that kept employees from Memorial Day picnics or Little League games.

That's why none of us could imagine anything less than a major catastrophe when our phones began ringing before the morning paper hit the ground on a sleepy Saturday in May. Speculation included a major lawsuit or our boss's sudden decision to leave the rat race and grow organic vegetables in Iowa. All of us were in the conference room by 7:00 A.M. As Marc stood to speak, I noticed that one side of his shirt collar was unbuttoned—a lapse I had never seen in my six years with the company.

"I want to get right to the point this morning," he began, with none of the usual playfulness in his voice. "We have been given an unprecedented opportunity and I need to know if you are willing to accept the challenge. It will mean a radical departure from our past working schedule and, I believe, a total commitment of time and energy."

Of the ten around the table, a few of us scribbled notes while the others massaged lumps of ever-present Play-Doh—the symbol of Wesson & Smith's commitment to approach everything through the right brain.

"A client wants us to design and implement a delivery system for his message," Marc continued. "Once it's in place and operating, we have no further responsibility."

"What's the message?" Candi Stevens asked.

"We don't have to create the message this time," Marc replied. "Just deliver it."

"Demographics? Target audience?" Ron Emerson wanted to know.

"If you'll hold your questions, I'll try to wrap up the concept first," Marc said. Were those beads of perspiration on his forehead? On Marc Smith's forehead? Mr. Cool was sweating?

"I know you'll find this difficult to believe, but here it is, and it's all true. Our task is to deliver this message simultaneously to every person on the face of the earth. The message must be clearly understood. The system must enable continuous delivery twenty-four hours a day, from now on. We have an unlimited budget to accomplish this and there are no restrictions on the amount of money you can spend."

A few people began to fidget, anxious to conclude this unusual exercise in corporate humor so they could get home. There were lawns to be mowed, bikes to be ridden, burgers to be grilled. Marc was not a practical joker. Innovative, yes. Off-the-wall, no. But he was our boss and the ten of us around the table each headed a department.

"The people here this morning will comprise the entire project team. Your departments can handle the agency's present accounts."

Marc took a deep breath and continued. "If you accomplish the client's goal, you will receive $5 million. That's personally, for each of you. I'll be up-front in saying that my share is

$50 million. This will not strain the resources of the client. He is well able to pay."

All doodling stopped. Half-formed Play-Doh images sagged on the table. He was serious, and suddenly we all knew it.

"We have sixty days to get it done."

A full half-hour was devoted to expressions of disbelief. The task was absurd, and the money involved was outrageous. Only our confidence in Marc and our hazy awareness of *Fortune* magazine's annual list of the world's billionaires allowed us to finally accept the proposal as genuine.

Ron Emerson was convinced that the mystery person was a Saudi with lots of oil.

"Sounds like a fair sheik to me," he deadpanned.

Could we live with his puns for sixty days?

For $5 million each we decided to try. We called our families, put our lives on hold, and turned on the computers. Someone across the office fired a wadded sheet of paper toward the wastebasket in a high arcing shot that was obviously too short.

"Airball!" Marc yelled as he caught it and flipped it deftly behind his back into the basket.

"Marrrrrc Smith, he's our man," Ron Emerson chanted. "If he can't do it, nobody can."

That spark of the old Wesson & Smith spirit raised my hopes for the moment. *Maybe we* can *pull it off,* I thought. *Just maybe.*

As a prototype we selected the country of Kenya in East Africa and gave ourselves two days to devise a plan. With about the same land area as Texas and a very diverse population, Kenya was a good test. Information poured from computer data bases telling us that English and Swahili would reach most people in the cities, but there were some forty ethnic groups, each with its own local language and dialect. Millions of rural people spoke only their tribal tongue. After two days, we hadn't adequately defined the problem, much less formulated a solution.

We began thinking of conventional methods like leaflet drops from helicopters, airborne loudspeakers, and even human messengers to each village. But we could not guarantee that these methods would reach everyone. The complexity of language and culture in just one African country was unbelievable.

Candi suggested we leapfrog the language barrier by using drama. "Why not pantomime the message on television?" she asked between spoons of yogurt during yet another working lunch. A satellite footprint covered all of Kenya but receivers were limited in the cities and non-existent in rural areas. With unlimited resources we could litter the country with satellite dishes and microwave relay transmitters. We could give every person a handheld TV set. But could we purchase and distribute them in sixty days? How long could battery power sustain the ongoing, twenty-four-hour delivery requirement? Radios were easier, but how could we be sure they would be turned on all day and night? Who wanted to hear an endless, ongoing message?

Fourteen days into the project, our individual two-hundred-dollar-a-night hotel suites felt small and our families seemed a million miles away. "Total commitment," Marc reminded us. "Pretend you're in Europe and call home once a week. This project isn't like pitching horseshoes. Close doesn't count. It's either $5 million or zero."

It must have been the jalapeno pizza for supper one night that fueled sci-fi visions of giant screens towed behind circling drones. Wouldn't the Kenyan government just love a few hundred unmanned aircraft buzzing around its airspace?

Politics! How could we have forgotten? A person could wander around the United States giving away TV sets or hauling messages through the sky, but not in most developing nations. One knowledgeable consultant laughed at any consideration of blanketing Kenya with our client's message, no matter what it was. "You people are very simplistic," he said. "In Africa, everything is political."

We spent a month on Kenya alone and finally hit the wall at 9:00 on a Friday night. Candi Stevens, the pride of the self-help seminar circuit, lit her first cigarette in six years and said simply, "There's no way."

The problem was not money—we had all we needed. Even the sixty days retreated into the background as an issue. With all the time in the world, we still couldn't make it happen. If we couldn't do it in one country, there was no sense thinking about the entire world.

"Humanly impossible," Ron Emerson muttered. "I'm going home, get a good night's sleep, and reapply for admission to the human race. Who's going to tell Marc?"

"I think he already knows," Candi said. She stubbed out her half-smoked cigarette and mumbled a curse.

When we turned out the lights and locked the front door, Marc was sitting in his office, staring at a computer screen-saver—little digital points of light winking randomly in a dark electronic sky.

PSALM 19:1–4

The heavens declare the glory of God;
   the skies proclaim the work of his hands.
Day after day they pour forth speech;
   night after night they display knowledge.
There is no speech or language
   where their voice is not heard.
Their voice goes out into all the earth,
   their words to the ends of the world.

ROMANS 1:20

Since the creation of the world God's invisible qualities—his eternal power and divine nature—have been clearly seen, being understood from what has been made, so that men are without excuse.

THE MAN WHO DID IT ALL

IT WAS THE BOOK the nation couldn't wait to read. To be sure, we'd seen "How I Made a Million" stories and "tell-all" memoirs before, but never like this. While other people had amassed fortunes and reveled in sensual excesses, all had experienced limits to their indulgence. This would be the inside story from the man who had done it all.

Some of it was already known. The business part was public knowledge—a matter of documented history. You didn't have to be an MBA to find it intriguing. There was a foreign trade agreement sealed by a marriage of convenience; a prosperous multinational corporation whose competitors sank into bankruptcy and chaos; stock-splits so frequent that analysts called the company "Amoeba, Inc." This man's legendary savvy in business and politics brought foreign heads of state to visit him while ignoring the president. Besides achieving monetary success, the man was a creative genius. He wrote symphonies, designed his palatial homes, and renewed the environment with parks, gardens, and fields. He made the long-told fables of wealth and power pale in comparison. He simply had it all.

The rumors about his relationships with women had circulated for years, but security leaks from his closest aides just didn't happen. To a population that thrived on explicit details about prominent people, those rumors simply weren't enough. Finally, for reasons known only to himself, he decided to tell it all.

The publishers tantalized the populace with pre-release blurbs like: "Anything I wanted, I took" and "No pleasure denied." With the promise of no reserve and no restraint, the world couldn't wait for the intimate description from the man himself.

The long-awaited day finally arrived with advance buyers watching their mailboxes and hopefuls lining up outside bookstores. With tightly gripped copies in hand, men and women rushed home to devour the contents in private.

I prevailed on a kind secretary to get my copy while she collected hers at the shop around the corner. "For my sister," I lied weakly, handing her the required thirty dollars in cash.

On the way home from work, I could see scattered copies being eagerly read by men and women alike on the commuter train. But there was no discussion of the contents. As usual, no one talked. I was a bit embarrassed to have a copy in my briefcase, and I wasn't about to take it out in public. I feigned disinterest and worked a crossword puzzle all the way from downtown to my stop.

Once inside the condo, I grabbed a cold soda and flopped down in the big easy chair. Now I could reward my patience and read it all. I opened the cover, read the first paragraph, and stopped cold. Was this some kind of joke? I never expected *that* for an opening.

☼

The words of the Teacher, son of David, king in Jerusalem:
"Meaningless! Meaningless!"
  says the Teacher.
"Utterly meaningless!
  Everything is meaningless."
What does man gain from all his labor
  at which he toils under the sun?
Generations come and generations go,
  but the earth remains forever.
The sun rises and the sun sets,
  and hurries back to where it rises.
The wind blows to the south
  and turns to the north;
round and round it goes,
  ever returning on its course.
All streams flow into the sea,
  yet the sea is never full.
To the place the streams come from,
  there they return again.
All things are wearisome,
  more than one can say.
The eye never has enough of seeing,
  nor the ear its fill of hearing.
What has been will be again,
  what has been done will be done again;
  there is nothing new under the sun.

Is there anything of which one can say,
  "Look! This is something new"?
It was here already, long ago;
  it was here before our time.
There is no remembrance of men of old,
  and even those who are yet to come
will not be remembered
  by those who follow.

I, the Teacher, was king over Israel in Jerusalem. I devoted myself to study and to explore by wisdom all that is done under heaven. What a heavy burden God has laid on men! I have seen all the things that are done under the sun; all of them are meaningless, a chasing after the wind.

BIG-TIME DROPOUT

IT WAS A STUPID MISTAKE, really, and a big one, too. Why did I do it? I don't think I really know. There are a lot of things about it I can't explain to anyone—even myself. I suppose it was a shortcut, just something I thought I had to do at the time.

In the absence of any statement from me, there has been a lot of speculation about exactly what I did and why. You see, there's nothing quite as disconcerting as a failure with no adequate explanation. Whether it's a beautiful movie star who takes her own life or a trusted church treasurer who steals from the benevolence fund, people wonder why. What made them do it?

I'm not sure I can tell you why I failed, but I want to set the record straight about what actually happened.

First, you need to understand something about my family. After my mother was transformed by a religious experience, our home became the unofficial headquarters and hotel for the people with whom she was involved. Our big house bulged with people all the time—people praying, eating, talking, laughing. They sat at our table, helped me with my homework, and shot baskets with me out in the driveway. They were the friendliest, most genuine men and women I'd ever known. Because I was a young teenager with no dad at home, they made a major impression on me.

And then my uncle Joe brought Craig Wilson to our house. He had become front-page news with his political fall from grace, and the nightly TV coverage followed every development of his federal indictments. When he said he'd become a born-again Christian, everyone thought it was a sham to avoid prosecution. But not my ever-trusting uncle, who brought Craig over for hamburgers one Friday night.

After supper the two of them talked for hours. Instead of heading upstairs to play Nintendo, I sat out of sight around the corner and listened to everything they said. After that evening, nothing seemed quite as important to me as it had before. I wanted to be like them and was ready to do whatever it took to follow God in their footsteps.

Just after my high-school graduation Uncle Joe invited me to postpone college for a year and travel overseas with him. He and Craig were going to do some teaching and preaching and wanted me to come along and help. Unbelievable! It took me about two seconds to say yes and start packing my suitcase. A month later we were on a 747 headed for places I had only heard about before.

After three exciting weeks, the adventure of being a missionary ended pretty quickly and things got tough. Craig became very ill and the whole enterprise ground to a miserable halt in a noisy, polluted Third-World city where I couldn't speak a word of the language. While my uncle tried day after day to change flights and reschedule meetings, I was stuck in a cheap hotel room with Craig who was wracked by vomiting and diarrhea. It wasn't my concept of changing the world for Christ.

I'm embarrassed to tell you how quickly I quit and came home. It didn't make sense to suffer when I could get myself out of it so easily. I thought my uncle and Craig would see the wisdom of heading home if I led the way. I bailed out, but they pressed on.

You see, I didn't think I was turning my back on the Lord, but I guess I was. Somehow, I couldn't trust God for the unknown things ahead.

So, I blew it. It was a tough way to learn, but I'm beginning to understand some things more clearly.

I thought that with a good family background, a great heritage of faith, and the most dynamic role models, my success was assured. But it all came down to my personal choices. For me, the issue was "Who's going to call the shots in my life—God or me?" Well, I called the shot and it was an airball.

I also learned some things about trust. It takes a long time to build trust but it can be destroyed in a moment. Uncle Joe and Craig depended on me. They gave me a great opportunity and responsibility—but I let them down.

It took years for me to accept the idea that my failure didn't have to be final. A friend back home helped me understand that. He'd been down a similar road and discovered that God's grace was bigger than his mistakes. "You can be like Judas or like Peter," he told me. "Peter denied Jesus three times, but he didn't just run away after he failed. He came back and Jesus forgave him. Judas pushed it all down inside himself. In his depression, he took his own life."

I'd been looking at my failure, at my lost opportunity, and asking, "What would have happened if I'd stayed, instead of deserting Craig and Uncle Joe?" I agonized over that for a long time.

Finally, I realized I could never know the answer to "What would have happened?" It was the wrong question.

The right question was, "What will happen if I follow Jesus and obey Him today?" I began to do just that and God changed me in ways I never thought possible. It happened slowly, over time, but it began with that decision.

My conclusion is that God doesn't look for the heroes who have never failed. He looks for people who ask His forgiveness and pick up where they left off with Him.

And pardon me for not introducing myself earlier. My name's John, but most people call me Mark.

ACTS 12:5–12 (APRIL, A.D. 44)

Peter was kept in prison, but the church was earnestly praying to God for him.

The night before Herod was to bring him to trial, Peter was sleeping between two soldiers, bound with two chains, and sentries stood guard at the entrance. Suddenly an angel of the Lord appeared and a light shone in the cell. He struck Peter on the side and woke him up. "Quick, get up!" he said, and the chains fell off Peter's wrists.

Then the angel said to him, "Put on your clothes and sandals." And Peter did so. "Wrap your cloak around you and follow me," the angel told him. Peter followed him out of the prison, but he had no idea that what the angel was doing was really happening; he thought he was seeing a vision. They passed the first and second guards and came to the iron gate leading to the city. It opened for them by itself, and they went through it. When they had walked the length of one street, suddenly the angel left him.

Then Peter came to himself and said, "Now I know without a doubt that the Lord sent his angel and rescued me from Herod's clutches and from everything the Jewish people were anticipating."

When this had dawned on him, he went to the house of Mary the mother of John, also called Mark, where many people had gathered and were praying.

ACTS 12:25–13:5, 13 (SPRING, A.D. 47)

When Barnabas and Saul had finished their mission, they returned from Jerusalem, taking with them John, also called Mark.

In the church at Antioch there were prophets and teachers: Barnabas, Simeon called Niger, Lucius of Cyrene, Manaen (who had been brought up with Herod the tetrarch) and Saul. While they were worshiping the Lord and fasting, the Holy Spirit said, "Set apart for me Barnabas and Saul for the work to which I have called them." So after they had fasted and prayed, they placed their hands on them and sent them off.

The two of them, sent on their way by the Holy Spirit, went down to Seleucia and sailed from there to Cyprus. When they arrived at Salamis, they proclaimed the word of God in the Jewish synagogues. John was with them as their helper. . . .

From Paphos, Paul and his companions sailed to Perga in Pamphylia, where John left them to return to Jerusalem.

ACTS 15:36–38 (SUMMER, A.D. 50)

Some time later Paul said to Barnabas, "Let us go back and visit the brothers in all the towns where we preached the word of the Lord and see how they are doing." Barnabas wanted to take John, also called Mark, with them, but Paul did not think it wise to take him, because he had deserted them in Pamphylia and had not continued with them in the work.

COLOSSIANS 4:10 (EARLY, A.D. 62)

My fellow prisoner Aristarchus sends you his greetings, as does Mark, the cousin of Barnabas. (You have received instructions about him; if he comes to you, welcome him.)

2 TIMOTHY 4:9–11 (SEPTEMBER, A.D. 67)

Do your best to come to me quickly, for Demas, because he loved this world, has deserted me and has gone to Thessalonica. . . . Get Mark and bring him with you, because he is helpful to me in my ministry.

♠

THE SCHOOL SOLUTION

Here lie the bones of Lieutenant Jones,
The pride of the institution.
He died one night in a firefight,
While using the school solution.

JIM TRIED TO CHUCKLE but managed only a grunt as those words came back to him. How long had it been since he'd first seen that little verse scrawled on a latrine wall at Fort Benning? Twenty years? Thirty? It seemed longer.

The school solution. The proper tactical approach to every battlefield situation. There were right and wrong responses to every combination of events. How could he have made the worst of the possible military choices on this particular day?

And how had he ended up back in a combat command after all those quiet years on the ranch in Montana? When he got back from Vietnam and settled down to raising cattle and a family, a national crisis was the farthest thing from his mind. The Army Reserve was a few extra dollars for one weekend a month and two weeks every summer. The best laid plans of mice and men . . .

He stabbed at the ground with a crooked stick. He had to bring his mind back to the reality of the situation at hand.

"Think, Jim, think," he urged himself.

He knew the enemy's tactics well. He had studied them, rehearsed them, dreamed them, lived with them for years.

He knew that retracing his own steps was poor military strategy, so why had he thought it would work? The enemy commander must have scratched his head then laughed aloud when he received the intelligence report on their current position. Jim knew his own forces were now in a fatal predicament and that he had led them here. He suspected it wouldn't be long until everyone on both sides knew it too.

That's what made the current situation so absurd. He'd smelled the trap a mile away and still led his entire force straight into it. What had he been thinking? Where was his mind? Who was he listening to? Certainly not to reason, nor to General George S. Patton.

Jim glanced at the sky, estimating the cloud ceiling at no more than three hundred feet and falling rapidly. Air superiority was a joke in weather like this. With uncrossable terrain behind him and the advancing enemy in front, Jim was out-numbered, out-flanked, and out-maneuvered.

Soon, Congress would be calling for his head. They had little patience with commanders who couldn't produce victory. No matter. His head would roll, but not at the hands of his own people.

Now, the enemy commander he had defeated so many times before would gain great personal pleasure by watching the decimation of an entire division because of a stupid mistake. Jim was sure orders had already been issued to take him alive. He would be paraded through the streets, insulted, imprisoned, and then . . .

Dust clouds and a distant rumble signaling the enemy's advance drew Jim's attention toward the horizon. He studied the map again, looking in vain for an escape route that didn't exist. With their backs against the wall, all they could do now was wait.

His thoughts drifted back to Donna and the kids. Jim had married late in life and become a father when most men become grandfathers. But he loved those two boys like he had never thought he could love anyone. Kids had always been just kids until his came along. They were different.

"What if I'd . . ." Jim stopped before the question formed in his mind. Life was so full of twists and turns. A man could weave the web of his own mental destruction if he tried to answer all of his own "what ifs." Sure, the army had needed leadership, but why him? Where were all the younger officers? They were the ones who needed a combat command, not him.

This was their military chance of a lifetime. Step right up. Get your hero buttons. Earn your ribbons. Most men get only one war in a lifetime. If you miss this one, you probably won't get another chance. Be a combat infantryman. See the world through a peep sight. Fun, travel, adventure.

A young soldier approached Jim and saluted smartly.

"Sir, a number of the officers have requested a briefing on the procedure in case we have to surrender. They'd like to talk with you over by the mess tent."

Jim stared at the young man and bent the crooked stick slowly between his thumb and forefinger until it snapped.

"Procedures for surrender?" he asked.

"Yes, sir," the soldier replied. "Lots of people are wondering about it."

Jim mentally reviewed the options. Retreat? Retrograde operations? Those were actions to protect an army while it regrouped to strike back. Surrender? It wasn't in the book. He had never heard of it as part of the school solution.

"Young man," Jim said slowly. "You go tell everyone over by the mess tent to inventory their ammunition and get their men squared away in their defensive positions. We have neither plans nor procedures for surrender."

The young man gulped a "Yes, sir," gave a hasty salute, and trotted off in the direction of the smoky plumes rising from a field kitchen.

Jim walked slowly to his command tent, entered, and secured the flap against intrusion. He fell on his knees beside the cot and buried his face in his hands.

Tomorrow it would happen. By sundown of another day, there would be nothing left of him or his men for the world to remember.

My life, he thought. *Just one gross tactical error after another. God in heaven, please, please help us now!*

Jim rose from his knees and looked again at the map pinned to the tent wall. Something struck him differently than all the times he had studied it before.

"It's a long shot," he murmured, "the longest shot in the world. It's crazy, impossible, absolute suicide. But if it works, we might have a chance. If it doesn't, they'll enshrine me in the military hall of shame."

He took a deep breath and wrote out the order to be given to his brigade commanders. "No one has ever done this before," he said aloud. "And no one may ever want to try it again. This is definitely *not* the school solution."

♠

EXODUS 14:5–28

When the king of Egypt was told that the people had fled, Pharaoh and his officials changed their minds about them and said, "What have we done? We have let the Israelites go and have lost their services!" So he had his chariot made ready and took his army with him. He took six hundred of the best chariots, along with all the other chariots of Egypt, with officers over all of them. The LORD hardened the heart of Pharaoh king of Egypt, so that he pursued the Israelites, who were marching out boldly. The Egyptians—all Pharaoh's horses and chariots, horsemen and troops—pursued the Israelites and overtook them as they camped by the sea near Pi Hahiroth, opposite Baal Zephon.

As Pharaoh approached, the Israelites looked up, and there were the Egyptians, marching after them. They were terrified and cried out to the LORD. They said to Moses, "Was it because there were no graves in Egypt that you brought us to the desert to die? What have you done to us by bringing us out of Egypt? Didn't we say to you in Egypt, 'Leave us alone; let us serve the Egyptians'? It would have been better for us to serve the Egyptians than to die in the desert!"

Moses answered the people, "Do not be afraid. Stand firm and you will see the deliverance the LORD will bring you today. The Egyptians you see today you will never see again. The LORD will fight for you; you need only to be still."

Then the LORD said to Moses, "Why are you crying out to me? Tell the Israelites to move on. Raise your staff and stretch out your hand over the sea to divide the water so that the Israelites can go through the sea on dry ground. I will harden the hearts of the

Egyptians so that they will go in after them. And I will gain glory through Pharaoh and all his army, through his chariots and his horsemen. The Egyptians will know that I am the LORD when I gain glory through Pharaoh, his chariots and his horsemen."

The angel of God, who had been traveling in front of Israel's army, withdrew and went behind them. The pillar of cloud also moved from in front and stood behind them, coming between the armies of Egypt and Israel. Throughout the night the cloud brought darkness to the one side and light to the other side; so neither went near the other all night long.

Then Moses stretched out his hand over the sea, and all that night the LORD drove the sea back with a strong east wind and turned it into dry land. The waters were divided, and the Israelites went through the sea on dry ground, with a wall of water on their right and on their left.

The Egyptians pursued them, and all Pharaoh's horses and chariots and horsemen followed them into the sea. In the morning watch, the LORD looked down from the pillar of fire and cloud at the Egyptian army and threw it into confusion. He made the wheels of their chariots come off so that they had difficulty driving. And the Egyptians said, "Let's get away from the Israelites! The LORD is fighting for them against Egypt."

Then the LORD said to Moses, "Stretch out your hand over the sea so that the waters may flow back over the Egyptians and their chariots and horsemen." Moses stretched out his hand over the sea, and at daybreak the sea went back to its place. The Egyptians were fleeing toward it, and the LORD swept them into the sea. The water flowed back and covered the chariots and horsemen—the entire army of Pharaoh that had followed the Israelites into the sea. Not one of them survived.

PSALM 66:5-6

Come and see what God has done,
   how awesome his works in man's behalf!
He turned the sea into dry land,
   they passed through the river on foot—
   come, let us rejoice in him.

PSALM 77:19, Living Bible

   Your road led by a pathway through the sea—a pathway no one knew was there!

MIDLIFE CRISIS

AUDIO JOURNAL. Taperecorded tidbits; talking to myself. For my ears only.

Wednesday—March 9

Resolved: Do things differently this year. I've earned it after all my time on active duty. It's time for me to start enjoying life. Besides, I'm not actually retiring from military leadership—just changing hats. From field commander to commander-in-chief.

War is a young man's game. Let some of those young turks get shot at. Gives them a new perspective on life. I've had all the battlefield insight I need.

As I told the VFW Convention earlier this week, "Victory abroad depends on stability at home. Veterans deserve good jobs." They loved it. Gave me a standing ovation. I'll take care of the government at home this time. Let someone else take care of the war.

Rank has its privileges, and so does political office. People expect me to enjoy my perks. I'd be a fool not to.

Friday—March 18
Beautiful evening tonight. City lights twinkle down below. Just back from a walk around the penthouse enjoying the cool air and the view. Speaking of the view, it was a bit careless of my new neighbor not to draw her curtains. Where has *she* been all my life? Unborn for much of it, I suppose. But is she a work of art! Can't I admire art?

What a paradox, this blend of opportunity and restraint. I spend my prime years gazing at stars from war zones, concerned for God and country, and find myself transfixed by her on this midlife night.

So, forget it. Forget her. Nose to the grindstone, shoulder to the wheel, ear to the ground. Duty, honor, self-discipline . . . hunger.

Monday—March 21
Woke up Saturday, Sunday, and today thinking about her. Finally told Carlton to find out who she is. It's nice to have one discreet aide who won't go running to the press to sell the latest gossip about me.

Tuesday—March 22, 11:00 A.M.
Didn't sleep well again last night—thinking about *her*. A full agenda of decisions to make and here I sit, consumed with only one. A lifetime of holding back and asking, "How could I?" is suddenly swallowed by an overwhelming, "Why shouldn't I?"

Wednesday—March 23, 10:00 P.M.

Good old Carlton works quickly. When his report arrived early this afternoon I promptly canceled my meeting with the treasury secretary and devoured every page and every photo of her.

So she's married—to Captain Alan Miller, one of my company commanders who's away becoming a military hero. He may even become a dead one. She could be lonely with him away.

Get a grip! I can't think this way. But why is the whole idea of right and wrong being overruled by a sense of urgent need, desire, and . . . yes, maybe there is something I have to prove to myself. . . .

Just phoned Carlton and told him to invite her to a dinner on Saturday evening. "The honor of your presence is requested . . ." I don't think she'll refuse. We won't tell her it's a table for two until after she arrives.

Thursday—April 14

Three weeks since our first evening together. Another note from her today. We're starting to carry on quite a little correspondence—besides all the other carrying on. I love the fragrance of the paper, the fragrance of her words, the fragrance of her.

Friday—April 29

"Pregnant!" Her note this morning was only one word. Oh, God, what do I do now? I've got to think, be calm. Get a hold of myself. I held the note over a match and the word disappeared in the flame. If only the problem would go away as easily as her note. I won't panic. I'm in charge. I'll make a decision.

Sunday—May 1

Don't know why I didn't think of it immediately. Carlton sent the message this morning. We'll bring her husband back here as a courier of classified information. He'll bring the battle reports, brief me directly, and have a night at home before he returns to the front. That should take care of the problem.

Tuesday—May 3, 11:00 P.M.

Captain Miller arrived on schedule today, and we had a cordial meeting. His formal report and my usual military chit-chat. "We're all very proud of you. Keep up the good work." Right now he should be at home with his wife, solving my problem.

Wednesday—May 4, Midnight

Why isn't anything simple anymore? Miller spent the night at the BOQ last night—some gung-ho nonsense about not feeling right about going home while his men were in the field in battle. I can't believe it!

So, I had him join me for dinner tonight. He sat in the very chair she occupied for the first time a few weeks ago. Courtesy demanded that he empty his glass each time I filled it. He staggered out of here half an hour ago—undoubtedly on his way home to the little woman, I hope.

Thursday—May 5, 9:00 P.M.

Got to get some sleep tonight. This Miller thing has gone on too long. With a little luck it should be settled soon. The man is amazing. Last night he was drunk as a skunk and still slept at the BOQ instead of going home.

Today at noon I sent him back to the field with a written message to be personally delivered to Lieutenant Colonel Phillips, battalion commander. I know Miller won't read it. Anyone who spends two nights at the BOQ instead of going home to his wife wouldn't think of stealing a glance at a message to a superior officer. It's a short message, but it should do the job.

Basically, I ordered Lieutenant Colonel Phillips to put Miller where it's hot, then withdraw his support. Everyone will follow orders without asking questions. A few heroes will die and the army will win the battle because of their sacrifice. We'll give Captain Miller a posthumous award for valor.

Wednesday—May 11

Today's intelligence summary reported the death in combat of Captain Alan Miller. He was a brave man. Naive, but brave.

Saturday—July 9

Almost four months since this whole affair began. Today we had a quiet wedding and she was a beautiful bride—my bride. Some think the marriage was a bit sudden after her widowhood, but people always talk. Soon they'll come to see me as the good guy, stepping in to support and raise Miller's unborn child.

In a few months, the dust will settle, people will forget all about it, and we can get on with our lives. Give it a few years and no one will know or care what really happened.

My tracks are covered. My conscience is clear.

In the spring, at the time when kings go off to war, David sent Joab out with the king's men and the whole Israelite army. They destroyed the Ammonites and besieged Rabbah. But David remained in Jerusalem.

One evening David got up from his bed and walked around on the roof of the palace. From the roof he saw a woman bathing. The woman was very beautiful, and David sent someone to find out about her. The man said, "Isn't this Bathsheba, the daughter of Eliam and the wife of Uriah the Hittite?" Then David sent messengers to get her. She came to him, and he slept with her. (She had purified herself from her uncleanness.) Then she went back home. The woman conceived and sent word to David, saying, "I am pregnant."

So David sent this word to Joab: "Send me Uriah the Hittite." And Joab sent him to David. When Uriah came to him, David asked him how Joab was, how the soldiers were and how the war was going. Then David said to Uriah, "Go down to your house and wash your feet." So Uriah left the palace, and a gift from the king was sent after him. But Uriah slept at the entrance to the palace with all his master's servants and did not go down to his house.

When David was told, "Uriah did not go home," he asked him, "Haven't you just come from a distance? Why didn't you go home?"

Uriah said to David, "The ark and Israel and Judah are staying in tents, and my master Joab and my lord's men are camped in the open fields. How could I go to my house to eat and drink and lie with my wife? As surely as you live, I will not do such a thing!"

Then David said to him, "Stay here one more day, and tomorrow I will send you back." So Uriah remained in Jerusalem that day and the next. At David's invitation, he ate and drank with him, and David made him drunk. But in the evening Uriah went out to sleep on his mat among his master's servants; he did not go home.

In the morning David wrote a letter to Joab and sent it with Uriah. In it he wrote, "Put Uriah in the front line where the fighting is fiercest. Then withdraw from him so he will be struck down and die."

So while Joab had the city under siege, he put Uriah at a place where he knew the strongest defenders were. When the men of the city came out and fought against Joab, some of the men in David's army fell; moreover, Uriah the Hittite died.

Joab sent David a full account of the battle. He instructed the messenger: "When you have finished giving the king this account of the battle, the king's anger may flare up, and he may ask you, 'Why did you get so close to the city to fight? Didn't you know they would shoot arrows from the wall? Who killed Abimelech son of Jerub-Besheth? Didn't a woman throw an upper millstone on him from the wall,' so that he died in Thebez? Why did you get so close to the wall? If he asks you this, then say to him, 'Also, your servant Uriah the Hittite is dead.'"

The messenger set out, and when he arrived he told David everything Joab had sent him to say. The messenger said to David, "The men overpowered us and came out against us in the open, but we drove them back to the entrance to the city gate.

Then the archers shot arrows at your servants from the wall, and some of the king's men died. Moreover, your servant Uriah the Hittite is dead."

David told the messenger, "Say this to Joab: 'Don't let this upset you; the sword devours one as well as another. Press the attack against the city and destroy it.' Say this to encourage Joab."

When Uriah's wife heard that her husband was dead, she mourned for him. After the time of mourning was over, David had her brought to his house, and she became his wife and bore him a son. But the thing David had done displeased the LORD.

The LORD sent Nathan to David. When he came to him, he said, "There were two men in a certain town, one rich and the other poor. The rich man had a very large number of sheep and cattle, but the poor man had nothing except one little ewe lamb he had bought. He raised it, and it grew up with him and his children. It shared his food, drank from his cup and even slept in his arms. It was like a daughter to him.

"Now a traveler came to the rich man, but the rich man refrained from taking one of his own sheep or cattle to prepare a meal for the traveler who had come to him. Instead, he took the ewe lamb that belonged to the poor man and prepared it for the one who had come to him."

David burned with anger against the man and said to Nathan, "As surely as the LORD lives, the man who did this deserves to die! He must pay for that lamb four times over, because he did such a thing and had no pity."

Then Nathan said to David, "You are the man!"

SUCH A DEAL

VICE SQUAD, LACY HERE. Again? Where was she this time? Yeah, yeah, I know. We're working on it. Keep an eye on her. We'll do what we can."

Lacy tossed the receiver on to the phone cradle and lit a cigarette, squinting as the smoke curled up into his eyes.

"Another report on our 'investment lady,' " Lacy said to no one in particular. "Got to an elderly couple over in Riverside for $10,000 this morning." He gulped down the last mouthful of cold coffee from his mug and grimaced.

Rick Patterson glanced up from a dog-eared file folder. He was only thirty years old, half Lacy's age, but their furrowed brows looked identical. In a line-up of foreheads it would be impossible to tell them apart.

"How do you know it's the same person?" Patterson asked.

"Looks the same, feels the same, smells the same. I can tell," Lacy said, filling his mug from a steaming pot.

"So bust her."

Lacy sat down on the edge of Patterson's desk.

"It's not that simple, Rick. She hasn't committed a crime yet."

"Stealing $10,000 isn't a crime?" Patterson countered.

"She didn't steal it," Lacy said. "She hasn't left town either. We know right where she is. She advertises in the paper and has an office in The Financial Towers building. She says all the money people have given her is invested. Claims they'll be rich if they're patient. The people gave her their money willingly, she gave them a receipt and it's all legit."

"So why worry?" Patterson asked. "Go out and catch a real crook." The younger man rolled his chair across the scarred linoleum floor toward another file cabinet.

Lacy banged his mug onto Patterson's desk, sloshing coffee onto the worn gray metal surface. "Look, Rick, if this chick is for real, I'll eat my badge. No, I won't. I take that back. If she's legit, I'll hock everything I have, borrow what I can, and give it to her. You know what she claims?"

"I don't know and I don't care," Patterson mumbled, retrieving another folder from the file drawer.

"She says if you'll 'invest' $5,000 today, she'll give you back a cool quarter of a million in less than ten years."

"Didn't some politician's wife do that with frozen pork bellies or something in Arkansas?" Patterson grinned mischievously but Lacy refused the bait for an argument about politics.

"$5,000 to $250,000," Lacy said, ignoring the previous comment. "What percent increase is that?"

"I'm a cop, not a math teacher," Patterson replied. "The lady sounds like a candidate for the state hospital."

Lacy dropped his cigarette into Patterson's coffee mug. It sizzled, half-submerged in the murky grounds, as Lacy removed himself from the desk top and wandered toward the window.

"The biggest problem is that we've found three people who claim this woman delivers exactly what she promises."

"Come on," Patterson said, becoming interested for the first time in the conversation.

"That's what they claim, Rick," Lacy said. "We interviewed them in their homes yesterday. They ain't starving by any stretch of the imagination, and they all say my investment lady gave them checks for $250,000. We're trying to get a release on their bank statements right now."

"Listen, Lacy," Patterson said. "If this woman could deliver on a deal like that, and there are people around who swear she pays off, people would be standing in line to give her everything they have.

"You'd think so, wouldn't you, kid," said Lacy staring out the window. "You'd sure think so."

PROVERBS 8:1–21

Does not wisdom call out?
  Does not understanding raise her voice?
On the heights along the way,
  where the paths meet, she takes her stand;
beside the gates leading into the city,
  at the entrances, she cries aloud:
"To you, O men, I call out;
  I raise my voice to all mankind.
You who are simple, gain prudence;
  you who are foolish, gain understanding.
Listen, for I have worthy things to say;
  I open my lips to speak what is right.
My mouth speaks what is true,
  for my lips detest wickedness.
All the words of my mouth are just;
  none of them is crooked or perverse.
To the discerning all of them are right;
  they are faultless to those who have knowledge.
Choose my instruction instead of silver,
  knowledge rather than choice gold,
for wisdom is more precious than rubies,
  and nothing you can desire can compare with her.
I, wisdom, dwell together with prudence;
  I possess knowledge and discretion.
To fear the LORD is to hate evil;
  I hate pride and arrogance,
  evil behavior and perverse speech.

Counsel and sound judgment are mine;
    I have understanding and power.
By me kings reign
    and rulers make laws that are just;
by me princes govern,
    and all nobles who rule on earth.
I love those who love me,
    and those who seek me find me.
With me are riches and honor,
    enduring wealth and prosperity.
My fruit is better than fine gold;
    what I yield surpasses choice silver.
I walk in the way of righteousness,
    along the paths of justice,
bestowing wealth on those who love me
    and making their treasuries full.

PROVERBS 3:13–18

Blessed is the man who finds wisdom,
    the man who gains understanding,
for she is more profitable than silver
    and yields better returns than gold.
She is more precious than rubies;
    nothing you desire can compare with her.
Long life is in her right hand;
    in her left hand are riches and honor.
Her ways are pleasant ways,
    and all her paths are peace.
She is a tree of life to those who embrace her;
    those who lay hold of her will be blessed.

@

THE PREACHER AND THE POLITICIAN

STEVE COULD HAVE BEEN one of the greatest preachers of all time if he'd kept his nose out of politics. I tried to tell him a hundred times to stick with the gospel and leave prominent people to live their own private lives, but he never seemed to listen. Steve could have been ignored or even tolerated in the nation's capital if he had talked only about God. But he insisted on speaking out about matters of the boardroom and the bedroom.

Of course, Steve didn't start in Washington, D.C. Preachers seldom do. From somewhere in Nebraska he just began moving from one town to another, preaching in public parks to whoever would stop to listen. To everyone's surprise, a lot of people listened. For six months he worked his way across the country and hitchhiked into D.C. about cherry blossom time.

Maybe I should have said no when he called and asked to stay at our place. My wife, Diane, was dead-set against it, but Steve was my cousin. My mother had asked me to give him a hand if the opportunity ever arose, so I gave in.

His first day in town he wandered down to Lafayette Park, just across from the White House and gave a sermon at noon. Instead of hecklers, he drew about fifty interested people, more than a few in business suits. Within two weeks, his hard-hitting talks became daily fare in the park. When a reporter noticed several members of Congress in the crowd, Steve was on his way to becoming a news item.

It was obvious by Steve's lifestyle and his clothes that public opinion simply didn't matter to him. Strolling down Pennsylvania Avenue in jeans, a T-shirt, and sneakers, he didn't exactly look like he just stepped out of *Gentleman's Quarterly*. One local reporter dubbed him "the ultimate low-overhead evangelist."

The crowds grew day after day, and it was almost as if they were convinced he was right before they ever heard him. When they went back to work after one of his "in-your-face" lunch-hour messages, folks kept thinking and talking about what he'd said. He was getting through to people. Why he wanted to put all that in jeopardy, I'll never know. But when he confronted Patrick McKenna head-on, his days were numbered.

McKenna was a political appointee to the upper echelon of the White House staff. He was friendly enough during casual contact, but insiders knew he hadn't gotten to Washington by helping little old ladies across the street. In a typical, governmentally mixed metaphor, McKenna's friends credited him with the instincts of a shark and the disposition of a land mine. His enemies were not as kind.

McKenna must have heard Steve in the park before he invited him to dinner and a private chat. Steve returned from their first visit with mixed feelings. He described McKenna as a man with a fascination for the truth, but with no intention of following it. Still, he seemed drawn to Steve and kept inviting him back for long conversations. It would have been all right if they had stayed with theology or even politics. Unfortunately, Steve turned the subject to personal morality, or Patrick McKenna's lack of it.

Steve never changed his message just because a prominent person was in the audience. But I thought things should have been different when he talked face-to-face with one of the movers and shakers. It always seemed to me that personal conversation was the place for a little tact and diplomacy. Steve didn't see it that way.

"At some point," Steve insisted to me, "a man who wants to get serious with God has to stop playing games and begin to face the truth about himself. McKenna is living with his brother's wife, Claire, and that's adultery. Claire's teenage daughter is walking the same road of immorality as her mother. They're all violating God's law, and everyone is afraid to say anything about it."

I wanted to tell Steve to take it easy, but the words stuck in my throat. "Easy" wasn't in his vocabulary.

A few nights later, McKenna invited Steve to dinner again. Claire, her daughter, and McKenna hadn't finished their appetizers before Steve spoke his mind. When my preacher-cousin spoke of adultery and immorality, McKenna smirked and dabbed the edges of his mouth with a linen napkin. Claire called Steve names he wouldn't repeat to me, took her daughter by the hand, and stalked out of the room.

A few days later Steve was in jail. Oh, it appeared to be a routine arrest for disturbing the peace and illegal assembly without a permit. But I was pretty sure who was behind his being handcuffed and led out of the park.

For weeks he languished in a cramped cell until things came to a head at McKenna's birthday banquet—a taxpayer-funded stag party. The liquor flowed freely among the invited military brass and the captains of industry. McKenna was in high spirits, but his senses were dulled.

What happened that evening is still not clear to me. I wasn't there, and my only sources of information are a few banquet servers. Somehow, Claire used her teenage daughter to extract a promise from drunken Patrick McKenna—a promise he never would have kept if he had been in his right mind.

The next day I received a call from the police department telling me that Steve had died in custody. They gave me twenty-four hours to take possession of his body at the morgue. "Accidental death during interrogation," they called it. "Cardiac arrest while resisting restraint and attempting to escape." One look at his body told me the report was a lie.

When I went to the press with my story, they turned a deaf ear. "Too much speculation and not enough facts," they said. My friends told me to drop the whole thing and avoid trouble for myself. Sometimes I can't believe it really happened. Not to Steve. Not in this city.

Was it worth it, Steve? If you could do it over, would you still press the issue?

MARK 6:17–29

Herod himself had given orders to have John arrested, and he had him bound and put in prison. He did this because of Herodias, his brother Philip's wife, whom he had married. For John had been saying to Herod, "It is not lawful for you to have your brother's wife." So Herodias nursed a grudge against John and wanted to kill him. But she was not able to, because Herod feared John and protected him, knowing him to be a righteous and holy man. When Herod heard John, he was greatly puzzled; yet he liked to listen to him.

Finally the opportune time came. On his birthday Herod gave a banquet for his high officials and military commanders and the leading men of Galilee. When the daughter of Herodias came in and danced, she pleased Herod and his dinner guests.

The king said to the girl, "Ask me for anything you want, and I'll give it to you." And he promised her with an oath, "Whatever you ask I will give you, up to half my kingdom."

She went out and said to her mother, "What shall I ask for?"

"The head of John the Baptist," she answered.

At once the girl hurried in to the king with the request: "I want you to give me right now the head of John the Baptist on a platter."

The king was greatly distressed, but because of his oaths and his dinner guests, he did not want to refuse her. So he immediately sent an executioner with orders to bring John's head. The man went, beheaded John in the prison, and brought back his head on a platter. He presented it to the girl, and she gave it to her mother. On hearing of this, John's disciples came and took his body and laid it in a tomb.

This story is also recorded in Matthew 14:3–12 and Luke 3:19–20; 9:7–9.

THE GILDED WATER COOLER

A LARGE BUBBLE FORMED in the depths of the water cooler and slowly made its way upward, breaking the surface with a muffled bloop. Two men and a woman conversed over their cups.

"Be nice if *we* got to go to the mountains once in a while like the boss instead of having to hang around here and do all the work."

"Wouldn't it? Questions come up and he's never here to answer them. Everyone who has a problem wants to talk to the man in charge, and frankly, I'm sick of telling them to check back next week. Don't they have phones at that conference center? Why doesn't he return his calls?"

"Give him a break," said the third party. "He's already gotten us a better working agreement than we've had in a long time, and there's talk that when he gets back this time, he'll have an even better one—all down in black and white."

"I'm not any better off than I was five years ago," said the first. "I haven't seen or signed anything."

91

"That's right," replied the second, drawing another cup from the cooler. "The company cafeteria may be free, but the same thing day after day? I miss the old haunts and a little variety."

"You have something against low-fat yogurt, salads, and fruit—every day?" the woman asked in mock amazement.

"Humph!" the man grunted, tossing down his water in a gulp. "I could go for a hot reuben sandwich and a cold beer."

The brother of the absent manager entered the office and strolled toward the water cooler.

"Morning," the brother said. "This the meeting of the minds?"

"This is it," came a curt reply. "This is about the only place any decisions get made around here anymore."

Surlier than usual, thought the brother as he stepped toward the insular walls of his office.

"Any word from the divine Mr. M?" a well-watered employee asked.

"Nothing yet," the brother said. "But you know how those contract meetings can drag on. Imagine he'll send a fax when he knows something. Well, I'd better get back to work."

He withdrew, tired of defending his absent brother, tired of trying to manage a family business.

That afternoon, a few more disenchanted people gathered around the water cooler. "Why can't anyone tell me if he ordered the parts or not?" a man shouted. "If the line shuts down it's my fault. If we wind up with a double inventory of parts, it's still my fault."

"Consolidated Engineering says that without our main man's signature on the contract this afternoon, they'll cancel their order."

"I don't get it," a woman said. "We have fax, e-mail, cellular phones, FedEx, and the United States Postal Service, and all we get from him is silence."

The talk became more heated, the threats more concrete, the plans more radical. The more they talked, the more they forgot.

Somehow they forgot that the manager had hired every one of them out of a situation of personal difficulty. Many had been overextended with their creditors and heavily in debt. Some had been convicted of financial misdealings and sentenced to prison. Others had been only a step away from a similar fate.

They all forgot that they had been given a new start, including a profit-sharing plan and a generous stock option. In reality, they owned the company. But the more they talked and complained, the more complete their self-inflicted amnesia became.

No one remembers who came up with the idea to send out for pizza, but a little impromptu office party seemed just the thing to forget their troubles—a head start on the weekend. It all began innocently enough.

Before long, bottles appeared and soon the water cooler was up on a desk, its contents being mixed with fiery waters of another origin. They ordered more food and sent petty cash to the closest liquor store for additional spirits. The party was really cooking.

"You know," said one man, "if it hadn't been for this water cooler we never would have gotten where we are today. It was all those talks around the cooler that did it."

Laughter! Toasts! A tipsy song sung to the conquering water cooler.

Hands wavered toward glistening foreheads in mocking salutes.

"Present arms! We salute you, our fearless leader!"

More laughter. A demand that the manager's brother acknowledge the water cooler's role in their deliverance.

"Make him spray-paint it gold and salute it himself."

The brother, fearing for his own safety and eyeing the security guards who had joined the insurrection, yielded to the demands among cheers and toasts.

Why fight an unruly crowd? he said to himself. *Maybe we can straighten it all out over the weekend.*

The party was in full swing when the door opened quietly and the manager slipped into the room. He stood unnoticed, just inside the door, his face a mixture of pain and rage. He had planned a special celebration to accompany his presentation of the new contract, but now this. Would these people ever learn? In their cynical impatience with him, they had unknowingly traded Chateaubriand at the finest restaurant for pizza from a cardboard box. Somehow it seemed to symbolize their whole approach to life.

And the contract. Would they ever know what they had lost?

Half the people still didn't see him walk slowly across the room, tearing the new contract to shreds. But when he hurled the huge glass water jug against the floor, the party was over.

EXODUS 32:1–20

When the people saw that Moses was so long in coming down from the mountain, they gathered around Aaron and said, "Come, make us gods who will go before us. As for this fellow Moses who brought us up out of Egypt, we don't know what has happened to him."

Aaron answered them, "Take off the gold earrings that your wives, your sons and your daughters are wearing, and bring them to me." So all the people took off their earrings and brought them to Aaron. He took what they handed him and made it into an idol cast in the shape of a calf, fashioning it with a tool. Then they said, "These are your gods, O Israel, who brought you up out of Egypt."

When Aaron saw this, he built an altar in front of the calf and announced, "Tomorrow there will be a festival to the LORD." So the next day the people rose early and sacrificed burnt offerings and presented fellowship offerings. Afterward they sat down to eat and drink and got up to indulge in revelry.

Then the LORD said to Moses, "Go down, because your people, whom you brought up out of Egypt, have become corrupt. They have been quick to turn away from what I commanded them and have made themselves an idol cast in the shape of a calf. They have bowed down to it and sacrificed to it and have said, 'These are your gods, O Israel, who brought you up out of Egypt.'

"I have seen these people," the LORD said to Moses, "and they are a stiffnecked people. Now leave me alone so that my anger may burn against them and that I may destroy them. Then I will make you into a great nation."

But Moses sought the favor of the LORD his God. "O LORD," he said, "why should your anger burn against your people, whom you brought out of Egypt with great power and a mighty hand? Why should the Egyptians say, 'It was with evil intent that he brought them out, to kill them in the mountains and to wipe them off the face of the earth'? Turn from your fierce anger; relent and do not bring disaster on your people. Remember your servants Abraham, Isaac and Israel, to whom you swore by your own self: 'I will make your descendants as numerous as the stars in the sky and I will give your descendants all this land I promised them, and it will be their inheritance forever.'" Then the LORD relented and did not bring on his people the disaster he had threatened.

Moses turned and went down the mountain with the two tablets of the Testimony in his hands. They were inscribed on both sides, front and back. The tablets were the work of God; the writing was the writing of God, engraved on the tablets.

When Joshua heard the noise of the people shouting, he said to Moses, "There is the sound of war in the camp."

Moses replied:
"It is not the sound of victory,
it is not the sound of defeat;
it is the sound of singing that I hear."

When Moses approached the camp and saw the calf and the dancing, his anger burned and he threw the tablets out of his hands, breaking them to pieces at the foot of the mountain. And he took the calf they had made and burned it in the fire; then he ground it to powder, scattered it on the water and made the Israelites drink it.

SECURITY OR RISK?

O F COURSE I'D THOUGHT about quitting before. Anyone who's worked for the government has thought about it at one time or another. You get tired of the hassle, tired of the picky details, tired of being a cog in a machine.

But there are other considerations. Working for the government provides a great deal of security. It was especially true in my department. When times got tough, they were tough for everyone but us. No matter what the economy did, there always seemed to be more than enough money, above and below the table, to keep us living in the style to which we had become accustomed.

Oh, sure, sometimes it bothered me that I earned more than people I knew, and that I was getting it at their expense, but that's life, isn't it? If you divided it all up evenly, the same people would have most of it back by the end of the game.

A lot of the guys I had gone to school with resented me and my job. But they could have done what I did if they had wanted to. They made their choices and I made mine. While they sweated it out working overtime, I was home relaxing in the hot tub. As I said, there are other considerations.

Besides, the only sensible reason for quitting one job is to take a better one. It always made sense to me to stick with something, no matter how bad it was, until I had a better alternative in the bag. Food stamps, unemployment lines, and social services questionnaires were not my idea of the good life. Neither were newspaper want-ads, endless interviews with personnel directors, and rejections. Thanks, but no thanks.

I suppose I'd still be right there with the IRS if it hadn't been for him and his friends. Unaccustomed as I was to brown-bagging it in the park, the weather seemed too nice that day for the usual three-martini lunch at Jacoby's. I decided that sunshine, a bagel with cream cheese, and a kosher dill would do nicely.

I was sitting alone on a park bench when he asked if he could join me. How long had it been since I'd eaten lunch with someone besides the guys in the office? How long had it been since anyone had asked to eat with *me*? Perhaps my world had become more narrow than I'd realized.

In a few minutes, we were joined by an unlikely mixture of men bearing burgers and fries. A business suit, a butcher's apron, and the dirty jeans of a construction worker were all present. What followed was the most extraordinary conversation I had ever heard.

For an hour, I laughed and listened like never before in my life. The laughter came from somewhere deep inside me—a place I had never discovered, or else known long ago and forgotten. Instead of being couched in the superficiality of double entendres or golf jokes, it grew out of the reality of life. It was a laughter that left me feeling cleaner than before.

As these men talked, I said nothing. That was unusual for me, but somehow I felt there was nothing I could add to their conversation. I was skilled in talk of sailboats, tax evasion, and weekends, but they were conversing about life. Walking back to the office I realized that I had been so intrigued I'd forgotten to eat half of my lunch. A first for me.

Those impromptu gatherings in the park became more frequent. I found myself declining the expense-account meals my colleagues and I had raised to an art form. Instead, I opted for a nourishment of a different kind—a meal of the mind and heart that satisfied, yet at the same time, left me hungering for more.

A few months after that first lunch in the park, the man who had first asked if he could join me, the leader of our discussions, walked unannounced into my office. Right there, in front of God and everyone else, he asked me to leave my job with the government and come with his organization.

We had never discussed it before, although it had crossed my mind. I knew that working for him would plunge me from affluence to poverty overnight. Frankly, I wasn't ready to buy my clothes at K-Mart and drive a ten-year-old car. The few times I thought seriously about it, I dismissed it all as fantasy. My usual reaction was, "Why would he ever want me?"

When his invitation came that afternoon, I was startled.

Was it smart to leave everything I had worked for? The government's pension plan rewarded those who stayed around to retire, not those who quit. Did I want to sacrifice that? I had no real idea what job I was being asked to do, how I would buy groceries, or what the future held. Could I afford to take the risk, do something that appeared totally irresponsible, and take whatever came?

Could I afford not to?

MATTHEW 9:9–13

As Jesus went on from there, he saw a man named Matthew sitting at the tax collector's booth. "Follow me," he told him, and Matthew got up and followed him.

While Jesus was having dinner at Matthew's house, many tax collectors and "sinners" came and ate with him and his disciples. When the Pharisees saw this, they asked his disciples, "Why does your teacher eat with tax collectors and 'sinners'?"

On hearing this, Jesus said, "It is not the healthy who need a doctor, but the sick. But go and learn what this means: 'I desire mercy, not sacrifice.' For I have not come to call the righteous, but sinners."

THEY COULDN'T
HANDLE IT

WORLD HISTORY 213. A room full of college sophomores battled "the nod monster" and spring fever as Dr. Marsden tried to lure our attention toward lessons from the ages and sages. His voice droned out into the drowsy atmosphere of 1:15 P.M. on a warm April Wednesday.

"They were prominent, successful, dynamic men," the professor proclaimed, "who rose to the highest positions of leadership in their countries. People looked to them for direction—and got it! But the same tragic flaw took its toll in each of their lives. There was a common factor in their experience that none of them could handle. What's your guess?"

Allan Collins spoke up first. He always did.

"Maybe they couldn't handle the stress," he said. "Everybody's talking a lot about burnout now and midlife crisis, but those are probably just new names for things that have been around for a long time. Look at how much a president ages in just four years. That's all stress, isn't it?"

101

Allan always ended with a question. His mother probably told him once to end his answers with a question so he wouldn't sound like a know-it-all.

Dr. Marsden jumped on the question like a chicken on a June bug.

"Stress? You mean you suspect that underneath those cool exteriors there were Type A personalities lurking? Well, part of the problem could have been that they chose work over play, feasting over fasting, indulgence over exercise."

Dr. Marsden's comparisons always came as couplets in a series of three, and he loved to wax eloquent with alliteration.

"Perhaps stress played a part," the professor continued, "but it was not the real culprit. I don't think we could explain their fall from power as the cumulative effects of anxiety and apprehension. If anything, they responded well to pressure, using it as a springboard to success rather than a pirate's plank to destruction. No, it wasn't stress."

I watched the notes on Tommy Wyandotte's page dribble off into a squiggly line as his head nodded forward then snapped back. Linda McCully stifled a laugh and I used the occasion to glance at her and smile. She was beautiful, but way out of my league. Maybe if I'd pledged Sigma Chi instead of living in the dorm.

"How about foreign policy?" asked a voice behind me. Was it really Allan Collins again? It was.

"Don't international politics often spell doom for the man at the top?" Allan asked.

"Meaning what?" queried Dr. Marsden.

"Well," Allan said with a nasal twang, "a man can be a great mayor, senator, or governor, but when it comes to running a country and dealing with other world powers, maybe he reaches his level of incompetence and the people won't put up with it."

"There's some merit to that idea," the professor replied, "because in a global society like ours, the thermostat of our country is in someone else's living room. Foreign oil, currency exchange rates, and political instability in the Third World all affect our economy here at home. The old methods of regulating the temperature just don't do the job anymore."

Dr. Marsden was clearly enamored by his heating and air-conditioning metaphor.

"But," he continued, "in the case of the leaders we are considering today, it was not the inability to formulate and execute sound foreign policy that dragged them down."

For some reason, the discussion picked up at that point. Maybe it was because Linda McCully was the next to raise her hand. How anyone could be that pretty and that intelligent was beyond me.

"What about human rights violations?" she asked. "Many leaders have been overthrown by oppressed people in their own countries."

"A good observation," Dr. Marsden conceded, "but there is a cause of failure far more widespread than oppression."

Perhaps the sleep-inducing effects of the noontime submarine sandwiches wore off at precisely 1:27 P.M. Or maybe college students really can get interested in why a lot of men who should have kept it all together, somehow lost control of themselves and their countries. For whatever reasons, there was a lot of verbal speculation centered on the "tragic flaw" concept introduced by Dr. Marsden.

"Was it personal tragedy?" a young man asked. "Aren't a lot of men able to stand up to knockout blows in business or government, yet go down for the count when illness or death strikes someone they love? If a chain is only as strong as its weakest link, then maybe a man's life is only as happy as its unhappiest part."

It was beginning to sound like a contest of "top that metaphor." The theories continued.

"It could have been a retarded child, a shattered marriage, or an elderly parent who lingered and suffered when death would have been a relief. All those could sap the strength of a man before he knew it was gone."

"Perhaps," replied Dr. Marsden, "but none of those was the leech that sucked the lifeblood from the leaders in question."

What was it then? Everyone got into the act, even sleepy Tommy Wyandotte who guessed "a sagging economy, unemployment, recession, and depression."

Class became a verbal free-for-all.

Was it a country torn by rebellion and civil strife? A generation gap that wouldn't go away? A breech in governmental credibility or a lack of integrity that couldn't be overcome?

Was it an unpopular war? Hawks and doves sparring over the proper response to an international incident? Political correctness so stifling that no one could do or say anything right anymore? Diversity versus morality? Too many lawyers? Too much money? Overpopulation? Global warming?

Dr. Marsden waited until the guessing game waned before stepping back in. "It could have been any or all of these," he continued. "Many great leaders have gone down trying to handle only one of these issues, much less the tangled combinations that seem to be the norm today. But it was none of those you have mentioned.

"The single, common thing that each of these men could not handle is an enemy more subtle, more ruthless, more destructive than any we have yet considered. It is no respecter of persons.

"Like money, technology, or nuclear energy, it is a neutral commodity. Used correctly it has great power to give life. Abused, it kills with no conscience."

The bells in the library tower began to chime the hour and the sidewalk outside filled with students glad to escape from academia into a spring afternoon. I glanced back at Allan Collins and then at Linda McCully. No one in the classroom had closed a notebook or even moved.

Tommy Wyandotte held his Bic pen poised over a page of faultless notes, unmarred by squiggly lines.

"I have placed a dozen copies of the Old Testament on reserve in the library," the professor said. "Each copy contains bookmarks at four different places. Your assignment is to read each of the four selections before class on Friday."

The silence persisted.

"The common experience which none of these men could handle," concluded Dr. Marsden, "is the very thing each of you is here to find. If you gain it, I hope it doesn't destroy you. We call it—success.

"Class dismissed."

DEUTERONOMY 8:10-18

When you have eaten and are satisfied, praise the LORD your God for the good land he has given you. Be careful that you do not forget the LORD your God, failing to observe his commands, his laws and his decrees that I am giving you this day. Otherwise, when you eat and are satisfied, when you build fine houses and settle down, and when your herds and flocks grow large and your silver and gold increase and all you have is multiplied, then your heart will become proud and you will forget the LORD your God, who brought you out of Egypt, out of the land of slavery. He led you through the vast and dreadful desert, that thirsty and waterless land, with its venomous snakes and scorpions. He brought you water out of hard rock. He gave you manna to eat in the desert, something your fathers had never known, to humble and to test you so that in the end it might go well with you. You may say to yourself, "My power and the strength of my hands have produced this wealth for me." But remember the LORD your God, for it is he who gives you the ability to produce wealth, and so confirms his covenant, which he swore to your forefathers, as it is today.

First Kings 10:23–11:6 describes Solomon's downfall.

Second Chronicles 11:5–12:1 tells the story of Rehoboam.

Second Chronicles 32 records Hezekiah's inability to handle success.

THE RESIGNATION

CHARLES TILTED BACK one last time in the brown leather desk chair and scanned the photographs on the wall. Beautiful women and smiling children greeted his gaze. Their moments together, now frozen in time and framed in gold, had been genuinely happy, but fleeting. Few voters cared that he had been married three times. It had come to be accepted as an adult rite of passage. "Things change," society said. "People have to grow and get on with their lives."

Blended families had never been easy, but Charles' family was blended and neglected, left like a meandering stream to find its own course. While he tried to guide the country, his offspring from three mothers ebbed past childhood and were swept into the turbulence of adolescence.

There had always been too much work, too many people depending on Charles, too many decisions in a world threatening to unravel every day. "The kids will be all right," he told himself. But they weren't. All that had brought him to this morning.

Today he was stepping down in defeat from the highest political office in the land. It would have been different if Congress had wanted him out, if they had charged him with misconduct or called for his impeachment. He had enough skeletons in his closet to undo him if his peers had chosen to drag one out.

But he had lost in the political process. Overconfident and unaware, Charles had been defeated by his son. And that's what made the bitter pill even more difficult for him to swallow.

Charles rose and walked to the sixteen-by-twenty-inch photograph of a handsome young man standing next to a white Corvette convertible. Justin was not his oldest son, but clearly his favorite. Charles gave him the car as a graduation present for finishing law school. "Justin, Justin," Charles whispered. "First in your class, first with the ladies, first in your father's heart. Close and yet so far."

Charles started to take the photo from the wall but stopped in mid-reach. That's how it had always been between him and Justin. Almost, but not quite. Aim for a hug, and settle for a handshake. Try for "I love you" and say, "You played a great game" instead.

Charles' mind wandered back a decade to the afternoon his son, Curtis, from a previous marriage had raped Tina, Justin's teenage sister. Charles had been furious but meted out neither discipline nor love. "It's a family matter," he had reasoned. If we call the police, the public will know.

"So I missed that one by a mile," Charles muttered to himself. The depth of Justin's smoldering outrage had escaped Charles' notice, though everyone else saw it clearly. Charles realized too late that Justin perceived the lack of punishment as indifference. Over time Justin changed his view of his father from "indifferent" to "incompetent," and determined to solve the matter on his own.

"I should have punished the rape when it happened," Charles told himself. "If I'd been paying attention, I could have prevented it in the first place. Maybe Justin was right. If a man can't manage his family, how can he hope to govern a nation? My son beat me with the oldest campaign slogan in the world, 'Time for a Change.' "

Through skillful grassroots public relations and the promise of a leader who would listen to the people, Justin engineered Charles' political downfall. No one in the country doubted that after the next election, the son would sit in the father's brown leather chair and make himself at home in the very office where he had played as a child.

A voice brought Charles back to the present.

"Sir, it's time to go."

The president took a deep breath and followed his aide out the door and down a sidewalk lined with members of his staff. A smattering of applause followed Charles as he grasped outstretched hands and smiled woodenly at tear-filled eyes.

"Keep moving," he told himself. "Keep smiling."

Today even the press was strangely silent. No microphones were thrust into his face and even the cameras kept a respectable distance. This man, considered free game during his days in office, was now being granted a deference that was, more than anything else, like a funeral in nature.

On his order, the engines of the waiting helicopter had not been started. Today there would be no whirling blades and buzzing tail rotor to drown out whatever anyone wanted to say. In his self-imposed silence, Charles was determined to face the music, whatever it was.

Who could have imagined it would end like this?

2 SAMUEL 15:1–6, 13–14, 17–18, 23, 30

In the course of time, Absalom provided himself with a chariot and horses and with fifty men to run ahead of him. He would get up early and stand by the side of the road leading to the city gate. Whenever anyone came with a complaint to be placed before the king for a decision, Absalom would call out to him, "What town are you from?" He would answer, "Your servant is from one of the tribes of Israel." Then Absalom would say to him, "Look, your claims are valid and proper, but there is no representative of the king to hear you." And Absalom would add, "If only I were appointed judge in the land! Then everyone who has a complaint or case could come to me and I would see that he gets justice."

Also, whenever anyone approached him to bow down before him, Absalom would reach out his hand, take hold of him and kiss him. Absalom behaved in this way toward all the Israelites who came to the king asking for justice, and so he stole the hearts of the men of Israel. . . .

A messenger came and told David, "The hearts of the men of Israel are with Absalom."

Then David said to all his officials who were with him in Jerusalem. "Come! We must flee, or none of us will escape from Absalom. We must leave immediately, or he will move quickly to overtake us and bring ruin upon us and put the city to the sword" . . . .

So the king set out, with all the people following him, and they halted at a place some distance away. All his men marched past him, along with all the Kerethites and Pelethites; and all the six hundred Gittites who had accompanied him from Gath marched before the king. . . .

The whole countryside wept aloud as all the people passed by. . . .

David continued up the Mount of Olives, weeping as he went; his head was covered and he was barefoot. All the people with him covered their heads too and were weeping as they went up.

The complete account, from rape to retreat, is found in 2 Samuel, chapters 13–17.

THE MINORITY REPORT

C ALL IT A JUNKET, a boondoggle, a fact-finding mission, or whatever you like, the company's twelve division supervisors had been on it for over a month. The rest of us had been humdrumming around with business as usual while they were off to see the world. Some of us had reached the point where we didn't care if they came back or not. We were doing fine without them.

Our company wasn't the best outfit in the world to work for, if you know what I mean. There had been a time, a few years back, when working conditions had improved dramatically, but after that, there were a lot of ups and downs. For a few months, production would surge, the future would brighten, and then bingo, we'd be back in the pits. As predictably as a roller coaster, employee morale rose to the heights only to drop to the bottom again.

One problem with the corporation was that it couldn't decide on a permanent location. Oh, the chief executive officer had picked a spot years ago, but when it came to persuading middle management and the rank and file to move, his plan always got ambushed somewhere in the process. I think, way down deep, all of us thought he had the right idea, but when it came to packing up and facing the challenge . . . well, you know how that goes.

That's why he sent the division supervisors to evaluate the area of our proposed relocation. "Visit the schools and the neighborhoods," he told them. "Talk to the people, listen to the Chamber of Commerce, and study the competition. I'll stay here and when you get back, the company will accept your recommendation. Either we all go or no one goes," he said of the move.

The incredible thing was that the CEO could have given every one of us a pink slip, moved by himself, and started the whole operation again with new employees. But he refused to do it. He had an almost obsessive commitment to making the company go with the people who were already part of it—us. It was like he really cared about us or something, but we were so hung up on the problems, most of us never saw that side of him until it was too late.

When the supervisors finally returned, the CEO assembled the whole outfit for the report—employees, husbands, wives, kids, pets, the works. Maybe he felt this was his last shot at moving the operation and if we could be convinced, the thing would go. What a fiasco it turned out to be.

First, we got the good news. The new site truly was a beautiful place. The climate, the scenery, and the quality of life were paradise compared to our present location. It looked like a good place for business and a great place to live. The CEO's mouth turned up at the corners.

Next came the bad news. Our company had such a bad image among the locals, you could feel the hostility in the air.

They saw us as a threat to their very existence—the way a small-town drugstore sees Wal-Mart. If we tried to move in, they were determined to block us at every turn, from housing to education. All of us knew we were in for a fight and none of us wanted that. They were the big boys and they played for keeps.

In addition, our company had been in a hand-to-mouth mode for so long, struggling to meet every monthly payroll, no one was sure we could finance a move like this. What if we went through all the hassle of a move and then had no jobs?

Needless to say, the entire audience erupted in a chorus of moans, groans, murmurs, and "I-told-you-so's." The roller coaster of morale hurtled downward, and the CEO couldn't believe it was happening again.

But it wasn't over yet. There was a minority report to be heard. Two supervisors out of twelve saw things differently. To them it was all a matter of backing. The corporation's one majority stockholder had offered carte blanche support for this move. "With that promise," they said, "nothing else makes any difference. We can do it."

The competition, the threats, even the inertia of our own people were simply opportunities on which we could capitalize.

When the other supervisors asked the two dissenters to produce evidence of cash in hand or a line of credit from the majority stockholder, there was an awkward silence. They answered in simple confidence, "It's promised—when we need it. He's always come through in the past and there's no reason to think he won't come through again."

For a few minutes we wavered. But the optimism of two against the realism of ten wasn't enough to sway our naturally pessimistic people. The moans, groans, and murmurs prevailed and we voted down the proposal to move.

We could all do without the pain of relocation. The kids didn't need to be uprooted and exposed to unnecessary risks. For that matter, neither did we. Besides, it wasn't so bad where we were. Maybe not paradise, but comfortable.

Driving home that night, my wife and I shared a feeling of relief that the discussions were finally over. Jeremy, our four-year-old, clutched his ragged old doggie and said, "Daddy, are we going to move?"

"No, son. We don't have to move. We're going to stay right where we are."

"Was it a nice place where we might have moved?" he asked with a yawn.

"I don't really know, Jeremy. Some said it was and others said it wasn't. It might have been hard to live there," I said.

"I'm tough," he sighed and fell asleep in the back seat of the car.

My thoughts turned back to the meeting and the minority report. Yes, I was relieved. But somewhere deep inside me I wondered if we had just missed a once-in-a-lifetime opportunity that looked so much like a problem we did everything we could to avoid it.

Comfort or risk? We couldn't have it both ways. We made our choice.

Had we been astute or asleep?

NUMBERS 13:1–3, 17–21, 25–33

NUMBERS 14:1–24, 30

The Lord said to Moses, "Send some men to explore the land of Canaan, which I am giving to the Israelites. From each ancestral tribe send one of its leaders."

So at the LORD's command, Moses sent them out from the Desert of Paran. All of them were leaders of the Israelites. . . .

When Moses sent them to explore Canaan, he said, "Go up through the Negev and on into the hill country. See what the land is like and whether the people who live there are strong or weak, few or many. What kind of land do they live in? Is it good or bad? What kind of towns do they live in? Are they unwalled or fortified? How is the soil? Is it fertile or poor? Are there trees on it or not? Do your best to bring back some of the fruit of the land." (It was the season for the first ripe grapes.)

So they went up and explored the land. . . . At the end of forty days they returned from exploring the land.

They came back to Moses and Aaron and the whole Israelite community at Kadesh in the Desert of Paran. There they reported to them and to the whole assembly and showed them the fruit of the land. They gave Moses this account: "We went into the land to which you sent us, and it does flow with milk and honey! Here is its fruit. But the people who live there are powerful, and the cities are fortified and very large. We even saw descendants of Anak there. The Amalekites live in the Negev; the Hittites, Jebusites and Amorites live in the hill country; and the Canaanites live near the sea and along the Jordan."

Then Caleb silenced the people before Moses and said, "We should go up and take possession of the land, for we can certainly do it."

But the men who had gone up with him said, "We can't attack those people; they are stronger than we are." And they spread among the Israelites a bad report about the land they had explored. They said, "The land we explored devours those living in it. All the people we saw there are of great size. We saw the Nephilim there (the descendants of Anak come from the Nephilim). We seemed like grasshoppers in our own eyes, and we looked the same to them."

That night all the people of the community raised their voices and wept aloud. All the Israelites grumbled against Moses and Aaron, and the whole assembly said to them, "If only we had died in Egypt! Or in this desert! Why is the LORD bringing us to this land only to let us fall by the sword? Our wives and children will be taken as plunder. Wouldn't it be better for us to go back to Egypt?" And they said to each other, "We should choose a leader and go back to Egypt."

Then Moses and Aaron fell facedown in front of the whole Israelite assembly gathered there. Joshua son of Nun and Caleb son of Jephunneh, who were among those who had explored the land, tore their clothes and said to the entire Israelite assembly, "The land we passed through and explored is exceedingly good. If the LORD is pleased with us, he will lead us into that land, a land flowing with milk and honey, and will give it to us. Only do not rebel against the LORD. And do not be afraid of the people of the land, because we will swallow them up. Their protection is gone, but the LORD is with us. Do not be afraid of them."

But the whole assembly talked about stoning them. Then the glory of the LORD appeared at the Tent of Meeting to all the Israelites. The LORD said to Moses, "How long will these people treat me with contempt? How long will they refuse to believe in me, in spite of all the miraculous signs I have performed among them? I will strike them down with a plague and destroy them, but I will make you into a nation greater and stronger than they."

Moses said to the LORD, "Then the Egyptians will hear about it! By your power you brought these people up from among them. And they will tell the inhabitants of this land about it. They have already heard that you, O LORD, are with these people and that you, O LORD, have been seen face to face, that your cloud stays over them, and that you go before them in a pillar of cloud by day and a pillar of fire by night. If you put these people to death all at one time, the nations who have heard this report about you will say, 'The LORD was not able to bring these people into the land he promised them on oath; so he slaughtered them in the desert.'

"Now may the Lord's strength be displayed, just as you have declared: 'The LORD is slow to anger, abounding in love and forgiving sin and rebellion. Yet he does not leave the guilty unpunished; he punishes the children for the sin of the fathers to the third and fourth generation.' In accordance with your great love, forgive the sin of these people, just as you have pardoned them from the time they left Egypt until now."

The LORD replied, "I have forgiven them, as you asked. Nevertheless, as surely as I live and as surely as the glory of the

LORD fills the whole earth, not one of the men who saw my glory and the miraculous signs I performed in Egypt and in the desert but who disobeyed me and tested me ten times—not one of them will ever see the land I promised on oath to their forefathers. No one who has treated me with contempt will ever see it. But because my servant Caleb has a different spirit and follows me wholeheartedly, I will bring him into the land he went to, and his descendants will inherit it . . .

Not one of you will enter the land I swore with uplifted hand to make your home, except Caleb son of Jephunneh and Joshua son of Nun.

THANKS, BUT NO THANKS

G ENEROUS TO A FAULT." That's how everyone described my dad. He extended credit to customers in business, made personal loans to friends, and generally gave money away like it was ripe fruit on an overloaded backyard tree.

He lived by a simple motto, "If I have it and you need it, it's yours." Did people take advantage of him? Did they ever. Especially my older brother, Phil.

It started with a loan for Phil's first car and escalated from there. Every year he needed cash to "get through a tight spot" or "until things turned around." A house, a boat, a business, a divorce. On and on and on. So Dad made loans, gave gifts, and cosigned notes while Phil never seemed to care which was which. Consequently, I don't think my brother ever repaid a thin dime.

I made up my mind as a teenager never to presume on Dad's generosity. In fact, I had been on my own for years when I found myself in a real bind. With every other possibility exhausted, I turned toward home for help.

My fax to Dad asked for a $10,000 loan at the going interest rate. It was for my business, not a vacation, and I included a repayment schedule, just like I would with a bank. The next day, a check arrived by overnight delivery. Dad was amazing. And then I noticed the check was for $20,000—double my request. I should have known why before reading Dad's letter:

Dear Son:
Thanks for your fax. Always good to hear from you. Glad I can help in this situation. I always told you to "holler" when you needed help.
You'll notice that the enclosed check is for what you requested plus another $10,000.
Please accept your $10,000 as a gift from me to you, not a loan. You deserve a loan and I know you can repay it. But you're my son and this is the way I want to handle it.
I want you to give the extra $10,000 to your brother, Phil. It's a gift from me to him, just like the money I'm giving you. I know he can use it right now. All I'm asking is that you deliver it in person and tell him it's from me.
Love you both,
Dad

Why did Dad do things like that? I hadn't asked for a gift, just a loan so I could get over a temporary tight spot with a creditor. I was responsible and had every intention of paying it back. My deadbeat brother didn't deserve another penny, with his track record of squandering everything he'd already received.
My request was between my father and me. Why should I have to deal with Phil again?
Of course I understood exactly what Dad was up to. He knew how I felt about Phil. I hadn't spoken to my brother in

years and wasn't interested in breaking the silence now. So Dad answered my request way beyond what I asked, gave the same to my no-account brother, and put it all in one check. If I wanted my money, I had to give Phil's money to him—in person.

I thought about it for a long time and decided if that's how things were, I'd find the money another way or just do without. I didn't care what it cost to do it this way. I still had my pride.

With a red marker, I wrote VOID across the front of the check and added a little note before dropping it in the mail:

Dear Dad:

Re: your gift, thanks . . . but no thanks.

LUKE 15:11–32

Jesus continued: "There was a man who had two sons. The younger one said to his father, 'Father, give me my share of the estate.' So he divided his property between them.

"Not long after that, the younger son got together all he had, set off for a distant country and there squandered his wealth in wild living. After he had spent everything, there was a severe famine in that whole country, and he began to be in need. So he went and hired himself out to a citizen of that country, who sent him to his fields to feed pigs. He longed to fill his stomach with the pods that the pigs were eating, but no one gave him anything.

"When he came to his senses, he said, 'How many of my father's hired men have food to spare, and here I am starving to death! I will set out and go back to my father and say to him: 'Father, I have sinned against heaven and against you. I am no longer worthy to be called your son; make me like one of your hired men.' So he got up and went to his father.

"But while he was still a long way off, his father saw him and was filled with compassion for him; he ran to his son, threw his arms around him and kissed him.

"The son said to him, 'Father, I have sinned against heaven and against you. I am no longer worthy to be called your son.'

"But the father said to his servants, 'Quick! Bring the best robe and put it on him. Put a ring on his finger and sandals on his feet. Bring the fattened calf and kill it. Let's have a feast and celebrate. For this son of mine was dead and is alive again; he was lost and is found.' So they began to celebrate.

"Meanwhile, the older son was in the field. When he came near the house, he heard music and dancing. So he called one of the servants and asked him what was going on. 'Your brother has come,' he replied, 'and your father has killed the fattened calf because he has him back safe and sound.'

"The older brother became angry and refused to go in. So his father went out and pleaded with him. But he answered his father, 'Look! All these years I've been slaving for you and never disobeyed your orders. Yet you never gave me even a young goat so I could celebrate with my friends. But when this son of yours who has squandered your property with prostitutes comes home, you kill the fattened calf for him!'

" 'My son,' the father said, 'you are always with me, and everything I have is yours. But we had to celebrate and be glad, because this brother of yours was dead and is alive again; he was lost and is found.' "

HE LOVES ME NOT

" . . . no one knows what goes on behind closed doors."

Elizabeth switched off the radio and reached for a perfume bottle. Four quick sprays and the room was bathed in a fragrance that spoke of starlight and soft summer nights. At least that's what the cosmetic company claimed. At 10:30 in the morning, she was counting heavily on its sensory contribution to what she wanted to say.

She stood and gazed at herself in the mirror. She was thirty-seven years old by the calendar, but her face and figure had not released their claim on younger days. Heads still turned when she walked through a shopping mall or drove down the street. Her face was eye-catching enough to encourage a stare from any man.

She moved to her bedroom window, pulled the curtain slightly to one side and peered into the courtyard of her spacious home. There, almost within reach, a young man of perhaps twenty worked the earth of a flower bed. Sweat drops glistened on his bare back and ran down toward the waist of his Levis.

Elizabeth tingled inside. It was the same excitement she had felt the first time she realized that the boys in high school were watching her walk down the hall. It was an electric feeling she had learned to cultivate in herself and in others by the way she dressed and carried herself.

"But," she whispered to herself, "is that young man made of stone? Does he ever tingle? Let's try again and see if we can find out."

Elizabeth drew the curtains back from a sliding glass door, opened it slowly, and stepped into the courtyard. A cool breeze of air-conditioned fragrance rushed toward the young man and he hesitated slightly before pushing the shovel once again into the soft earth.

"Good morning, Nicholas," she said, approaching him from behind. "You'll have some beautiful flowers there in no time."

Nicholas turned around slowly, hesitantly.

"Yes, ma'am. I hope so," he said with a peripheral glance that confirmed their aloneness in the courtyard. She never seemed to appear when anyone else was around.

"Nicholas, the faucet in my bathroom is making a terrible noise. Could you take a quick look at it for me?"

"Uh, maybe Charlie could look at it this afternoon, ma'am. Would that be soon enough? I really do need to finish up this flower bed and then get the things ordered for your party this weekend."

Elizabeth pursed her lips slightly, then smiled. "If you could just come inside and take a quick look at it now, I'm sure you could fix it in no time."

Nicholas slipped on his shirt, buttoning it quickly as they walked toward the open sliding door. Inside, Nicholas entered the bathroom while Elizabeth remained in the cool fragrance of the master bedroom. He tried one faucet and then the other at the sink. The water gurgled quickly and quietly from both.

He moved to the tub and spun the sparkling handles one way and then back. No noise. He knew that when he re-entered the bedroom Elizabeth would be sitting on the bed in some alluring state of dress or undress. This wasn't the first time it had happened, and it probably wouldn't be the last.

She was one of the most beautiful women he had ever seen. During times of unguarded thought he often found his mind returning to images of their previous encounters and what might have happened if he had let it. Somehow she had selected him as a goal, a prize. And there was, he supposed, reward enough for him in being won by her.

No one would know. No one would care. Her military husband was gone most of the time and probably had his own extracurricular pursuits on the side.

Nicholas turned on a faucet and stared into the mirror. No one would know. No one would care, certainly not about him. He had been forced into this situation, an unwilling refugee who had to abandon plans for a promising future and accept the role of a servant in a foreign land.

He had done well here, learning the language, the culture, and earning promotion through faithful service. And now this. Again.

He turned off the water and walked into the room. Elizabeth had closed the curtain over the glass door and stood leaning against it. Her lips parted in a smile as he walked toward her.

"I'm sorry, ma'am. I couldn't find anything wrong with the faucets. I'll have Charlie stop by later and take a closer look at them. If you'll excuse me, I need to get on back to the flowers."

He stood waiting for her to release her hold on the door. Her hands reached up, gripped the front of his shirt and in a single ripping motion, tore it open and pulled it from his shoulders. He stood motionless for a moment, then quickly, forcefully, he reached for her.

Elizabeth's face registered a shocked smile as Nicholas grabbed her by the shoulders, spun her around, and threw her away from the door. She landed face down on the bed, still clutching his shirt.

Nicholas backed quickly toward the door.

"I can't," he said. "I've got reasons, the best in the world. I'm sorry."

He slid the glass door open and was gone.

Elizabeth rolled over, held his shirt to her face and began to sob and curse. But almost as suddenly as she had begun, she stopped. She stood up, unlocked the door into the house, ripped a sleeve off her blouse and began to scream.

As the servants rushed into the bedroom, she collapsed on the bed and sobbed out a story of attempted rape. She showed them the shirt and ordered them to call the police.

Nicholas was convicted on the basis of Elizabeth's testimony and summarily sent to prison. Late one afternoon, he stood looking out the barred window of his cell, contemplating his fate as the sun slipped below the horizon.

"It's a strange reward," he mused, "for doing the right thing. But maybe God knows something I don't."

He took a deep breath and lay down on a hard pallet.

As the sky darkened and began to speak the language of starlight and soft summer nights, an enslaved woman paced the floor of her palace while a free man slept soundly in a prison cell.

Joseph had been taken down to Egypt. Potiphar, an
Egyptian who was one of Pharaoh's officials, the captain of the
guard, bought him from the Ishmaelites who had taken him there.

The LORD was with Joseph and he prospered, and he lived
in the house of his Egyptian master. When his master saw that
the LORD was with him and that the LORD gave him success in
everything he did, Joseph found favor in his eyes and became his
attendant. Potiphar put him in charge of his household, and he
entrusted to his care everything he owned. From the time he put
him in charge of his household and of all that he owned, the
LORD blessed the household of the Egyptian because of Joseph.
The blessing of the LORD was on everything Potiphar had, both
in the house and in the field. So he left in Joseph's care everything
he had; with Joseph in charge, he did not concern himself with
anything except the food he ate.

Now Joseph was well-built and handsome, and after a
while his master's wife took notice of Joseph and said, "Come to
bed with me!"

But he refused. "With me in charge," he told her, "my
master does not concern himself with anything in the house;
everything he owns he has entrusted to my care. No one is greater
in this house than I am. My master has withheld nothing from
me except you, because you are his wife. How then could I do
such a wicked thing and sin against God?" And though she spoke
to Joseph day after day, he refused to go to bed with her or even
be with her.

One day he went into the house to attend to his duties, and none of the household servants was inside. She caught him by his cloak and said, "Come to bed with me!" But he left his cloak in her hand and ran out of the house.

When she saw that he had left his cloak in her hand and had run out of the house, she called her household servants. "Look," she said to them, "this Hebrew has been brought to us to make sport of us! He came in here to sleep with me, but I screamed. When he heard me scream for help, he left his cloak beside me and ran out of the house."

She kept his cloak beside her until his master came home. Then she told him this story: "That Hebrew slave you brought us came to me to make sport of me. But as soon as I screamed for help, he left his cloak beside me and ran out of the house."

When his master heard the story his wife told him, saying, "This is how your slave treated me," he burned with anger. Joseph's master took him and put him in prison, the place where the king's prisoners were confined.

But while Joseph was there in the prison, the LORD was with him.